The tree was almost finished.

'What do you say you and Beth put the fairy at the top together?' Matt lifted the fairy from her resting place on the coffee table and brought her over to Jack.

Carefully she guided Jack's hand, and fixed the fairy to the top of the tree. 'There! Now, we'll all close our eyes and make a wish.'

Jack squeezed his eyes shut, wishing hard. Beth's eyes met Matt's and caught in his liquid gaze. 'Close your eyes.' She whispered the words so quietly that she almost mouthed them at him. He had to have a wish. She wouldn't be able to bear it if he didn't.

He closed his eyes just in time. He didn't see her wipe the tear away as it dribbled from the side of her eye. And before he had a chance to open them again she had hastened back down the ladder and turned away, so that she could no longer see what her heart desired the most and what she knew she could never have.

Dear Reader,

This is a very special first for me. As I write this letter, I haven't seen this book in print yet. By the time you read it, I will have experienced the long awaited thrill of actually holding my first book. There will, however, still be one more thing for me to look forward to with grateful appreciation—the gift that you make of your time, in sharing Matt and Beth's story with me.

The book started life as an entry to the Mills and Boon Medical™ FastTrack initiative. When I first read about this ground-breaking new way of encouraging writers to submit their work, it seemed too good to be true. The offer of hearing back on a submission in days. And best of all, the possibility of receiving comments from an editor.

The shock and surprise when I received an email giving guidelines for improvements and inviting me to submit a full manuscript was profound. Then, after a learning curve that seemed almost vertical at times, self doubt and agonising hope, the unthinkable happened. The Call. The news that a book has been accepted for publication.

I knew what Beth was going to be like right from the outset—capable, good at her job and a gifted communicator. She's also determined not to be defined by the fact that she's deaf. One of the things I like the most about Matt is that he sees her communication skills as special, not just equal to his own, but different and better.

I hope you enjoy Matt and Beth's story. I'm always delighted to hear from readers and you can email me via my website, which is at www.annieclaydon.com

ALL SHE WANTS FOR CHRISTMAS

BY
ANNIE CLAYDON

First published in Great Britain 2011
by Mills & Boon, an imprint of Harlequin (UK) Limited.
Large Print edition 2012
Harlequin (UK) Limited, Eton House,
18-24 Paradise Road, Richmond, Surrey TW9 1SR

© Annie Claydon 2011

ISBN: 978 0 263 22445 0

Harlequin (UK) policy is to use papers that are
natural, renewable and recyclable products and made
from wood grown in sustainable forests. The logging
and manufacturing process conform to the legal
environmental regulations of the country of origin.

Printed and bound in Great Britain
by CPI Antony Rowe, Chippenham, Wiltshire

Cursed from an early age with a poor sense of direction and a propensity to read, **Annie Claydon** spent much of her childhood lost in books. After completing her degree in English Literature, she indulged her love of romantic fiction and spent a long, hot summer writing a book of her own. It was duly rejected and life took over, a series of U-turns leading in the unlikely direction of a career in computing and information technology. The lure of the printed page proved too much to bear, though and she now has the perfect outlet for the stories which have always run through her head, writing Medical™ Romance for Mills and Boon. Living in London, a city where getting lost can be a joy, she has no regrets in having taken her time in working her way back to the place that she started from.

**This is Annie's first book
for M&B Medical™ Romance!
Look out for more from her coming soon!**

The list of people who
deserve heartfelt thanks is a long one—
but my mum is not so well at the moment
so I'm sure no-one will mind if
she is first in the queue.

For my mother
who taught me how to read and write
and always encouraged me to do both

CHAPTER ONE

MATT SUTHERLAND was lost. The feeling had become increasingly familiar to him over the last few years and he did what he always did. Set his emotions aside, decided on a course of action and pressed forward. In this particular instance, the strategy didn't seem to be working and he was in danger of being late for his breakfast meeting.

The wide, cream-painted corridors of the hospital still looked as uniform as they had two weeks ago. He increased his pace to catch up with two women up ahead, walking companionably together, both loaded down with bags, coats and NHS standard issue manila folders. They had to be on the staff. Matt caught up with them, brushing the sleeve of the closest with his fingers, and she turned.

'Excuse me.' He spoke before he had taken a moment to look at her. 'I'm looking for Cardiology.' He stopped, suddenly aware of a pair of wide grey eyes looking up at him. Candid eyes, which looked directly and unashamedly at his face, making his lips tingle slightly as if he had only just remembered that they existed.

'You're on the wrong wing—this is yellow.' The other woman spoke up, pulling Matt's attention away. 'You need blue—the two wings have the same layout and Cardiology's in this location, only on blue wing. Go right to the end of this corridor, through the swing doors, turn left, then keep going until you get to Reception and follow the signs.'

'Thanks.' He turned back to the grey eyes of her companion. A distant, almost unrecognisable former self would have stopped and chatted, undaunted by any imagined consequence of charming her name out of her. Even now, a perverse, insistent voice at the back of his head made him try to goad her into speaking. 'So it's two parallel universes, then. Blue and yellow.'

She nodded. Her face was framed with dark curls and her half-smile struck him as intriguing rather than disinterested. A long-forgotten thrill ignited in his gut, and Matt reminded himself sternly that there was somewhere else he needed to be.

'Okay, thanks.' He'd got a reaction of sorts and found himself grinning in response. He cut his losses and hurried away, the cold gloom of a chilly December morning forgotten for the moment.

Turning, as if he wanted to check the direction, he saw the women behind him. They had stopped outside one of the entranceways in the corridor, their bags at their feet, and were facing each other, their hands forming words and phrases as they silently laughed together.

Nice one, Matt. Her gaze, so intent on his lips, had simply been so that she could see what he was saying. Regret tugged at a part of his consciousness that he thought he had left behind for ever and he turned on his heel, making for the reception area that he had walked through five minutes ago.

As soon as the stranger's back was turned, Marcie Taylor turned to her companion, a broad grin on her face. The sign she made with her hand was not for Beth's benefit, but so the man walking away from them could not hear her comment. *Nice!*

Beth turned to watch him hurry away, his dark

coat open and swirling around his legs, a gash of red at his neck from a bright woollen scarf. She twisted back to face Marcie before he had a chance to turn and catch her staring.

'Do you know who he is?' Marcie was still signing.

Beth shook her head. *'ID tags and a suit. He must be pretty senior. The new head of cardiology maybe?'*

'Must be. They say we were lucky to get him. Some hotshot surgeon from one of the London Centres of Excellence.' Marcie slipped back into speech now that the man was through the swing doors and safely out of earshot. 'Quite a catch all round in my opinion.'

Beth felt her colour rise and gestured a *'so-so'* with her hand, her fingers trembling slightly at the audacity of the understatement. 'Nice eyes.'

'And the rest,' Marcie retorted. 'If it'd been me on the end of that smile he gave you, I'd be on the phone right now, telling James that it was all over.'

'You'd do no such thing!'

'Okay, so I'm all talk. You couldn't keep your eyes off him, though.' Marcie's grin turned calculating. 'If he's new in town he probably won't know anyone. Do you think I should ask him to our Christmas party? If you're passing Cardiology, you could pop in and deliver the invitation. Just a nice, friendly welcome, eh?'

'Why would I do that? It's your party.' Beth assumed a look of injured innocence that wouldn't have fooled a child. Anyone with a pulse would have noticed that smile.

Marcie signed her frustration. 'Because that's what you're supposed to do with parties. You get to know people. Remember dating?'

Beth made a face, turning the corners of her mouth down. 'I remember your party last year. If that's what dating entails, I think I'll pass.'

'Ah, Pete. The man who put the *x* into *ex*cruciating. Anyone who thinks that my Christmas party is the right place for business networking and not slow-dancing with his fiancée…' Marcie stopped and bit her lip. 'I should have taken him out and shot him.'

A mental picture of Marcie, in a fabulous dress and killer heels, marching Pete out into the night with a shotgun came to Beth's rescue and she grinned. 'Would have saved him the trouble of working up that list of reasons for dumping me, anyway.'

'There was only one reason, and that one stank. Along with his timing.'

'At least he gave me ten days to work out what my New Year's resolutions were going to be. And in case you're wondering, they're going to be the same for next year. Stand on my own two feet and forget about dating for good.' A stranger's smile was no reason to abandon the two mantras that had stood her in such good stead for the last year.

'Just because Pete turned out to be a complete toad, doesn't mean that there aren't any nice guys out there.' Marcie's eyes softened. 'James, for instance.'

'James is married. In case you hadn't noticed.'

'Well, he wasn't when I met him.'

Beth chuckled. 'And you rectified that omission as soon as humanly possible.' She jerked her thumb in the direction that the tall, blond-haired stranger had taken. 'I'll bet you anything you like he's married, too.'

Marcie's gaze followed the direction of Beth's gesture. 'What makes you think that? Apart from the fact that you're hoping he might be because then you don't have to think about the possibility that he might be available.'

'He's got kids. No one without kids wears a scarf with a school name tag on it.'

Marcie threw back her head and laughed. 'Okay, Sherlock, you win.' She rummaged in her bag for a bunch of keys and unlocked the door to the audiology and hearing therapy unit. 'I'll ask him anyway. If he doesn't bring a wife along, you owe me coffee for a month.'

If Beth had decided not to go anywhere near Cardiology, fate, in the shape of a six-year-old boy with blond hair and blue eyes, seemed to have other ideas. She had found him wandering alone in the corridor outside the hearing therapy unit, dirt on his hands and the knees of his jeans and close to tears. After a halting start, a little gentle persuasion got the whole story out of him.

'So your dad works here?' Beth had bathed his hands and was dabbing them dry. 'What's his name, Jack?'

Jack's tears were forgotten now and he looked up at her proudly. 'He's a doctor and he works in the cardiology department—that means hearts.' Beth nodded, looking impressed. 'His name is Matt Sutherland.'

Beth's eyes skittered to the dark blue cashmere scarf that Jack had been wearing, which had struck her as slightly unsuitable for a child. 'All right, then, Jack, I'm just going to make a phone call and find out where your dad is right now and then we can go and find him together.'

The thought that he was married with a child gave Beth the perfect reason to ignore the thrill that accompanied any thought of the disturbingly attractive Dr Sutherland. A call to his secretary elicited his whereabouts and Beth got Jack back into his coat, gripping the boy's hand tightly all the way down to Outpatients. The receptionist nodded her through, indicating that Dr Sutherland was currently alone and pointing to the small consulting room that was his for the afternoon.

Beth stopped in front of the door and took a deep breath. This was stupid. Just knock.

'Should I do our special secret-code knock?' Jack was looking up at her seriously.

'Do what, Jack?'

'Our secret code. So Dad knows it's me. He knocks back with his secret code and I know it's him.'

The temptation was almost irresistible, but the new head of cardiology was unlikely to live that one down in a hurry. Beth pulled her face straight. 'No, probably not. You don't want everyone to know it, do you?'

Before Jack could answer she raised her hand to tap on the door. As she did so, it flew open and her knuckles almost hit solid flesh instead of wood. Snatching her hand away, Beth caught his cool, clean scent as Matt Sutherland started backwards.

Only Jack seemed undeterred by the abrupt introduction. 'Hi, Dad.'

This close, he seemed taller. And without his jacket, the sleeves of his crisp, white shirt rolled up, he looked broader as well. 'Dr Sutherland?' Jack's reaction had pretty much established that, but she couldn't think of anything else to say that was even vaguely appropriate.

'Yes… Yeah, I'm Matt, Jack's father. What's he doing here?' He was standing stock still, blocking the doorway, one hand on Jack's shoulder.

'Beth Travers. Can we come in?'

'Sorry… Yes, of course.' His eyes flipped rapidly over the empty waiting room behind them and he stepped back, motioning Beth over to a chair. Jack slid past him and ran to the revolving chair that sat behind the desk.

'Is this your chair, Dad?'

'Yes. Want to try it out?' He was watching Beth as Jack climbed into the chair, his expression dispassionate.

'I found Jack wandering on his own, outside Hearing Therapy. He told me that his day-care lady was knocked over by a car and that he'd been brought here with her in the ambulance.'

'What?' Matt spun round towards his son. 'Are you all right, Jack?'

Jack was ignoring him in favour of the contents of his desk.

'He wasn't hit by the car, but he fell over when his carer pushed him out of the way and there's a graze on his hand.' Beth kept her voice even, reassuring. 'He hasn't complained of any pain and doesn't seem dizzy or disorientated.'

The shock in his eyes had subsided and Matt was nodding to her as if he were taking a patient's history from a colleague. 'Thank you. Will you stay a moment, while I take a look at him?' He didn't wait for an answer and Beth supposed it was an instruction rather than an invitation.

He dropped on one knee in front of the boy, swivelling the chair around to face him. Without being asked, Jack pulled Beth's penlight out of his pocket and proffered it to his father. 'Are you going to shine a light at me?'

Matt took the penlight and flipped it on. 'You want me to shine it anywhere in particular?'

Jack leaned forward, jabbing his finger towards his father's eye. 'When you shine a light into someone's eye, the middle bit gets smaller. Con-con….'

'Constricts.' Beth supplied the word quickly and Matt turned towards her, the tenderness that was spilling from his face catching her unawares, making her wish she'd kept quiet.

Matt shot her a grin and returned to his son. 'Do you know what makes them get bigger again? That's called dilating.'

'When you're in the dark. Beth showed me. Her eyes do it, too.'

Matt laughed quietly. 'I imagine they do.' He shaded Jack's face from the overhead lights with his hand, checking his pupils quickly with the penlight. 'That looks good. Shall I ask you some questions as well?'

Jack thought for a moment. 'I didn't hit my head when I fell over. And nothing hurts. I told Beth that already.'

'Well, that's good to know. Anything else?' As

he was speaking he was easing the boy out of his coat, checking him for any signs of injury as he went, his manner so casual that Jack hardly seemed to notice.

'I have a minor abrasion on my hand.' He held out his grazed palm for his father to see.

'Do you now? Well, I'm glad you remembered that.' He shone the light from the pen torch onto Jack's hand and studied it closely. 'Well, I think you'll live, mate. We'll put some antiseptic cream on it, just to make sure it heals nicely.' He flipped the penlight quickly towards his son and Jack caught it adroitly. There was nothing wrong with the boy's reactions.

Matt seemed satisfied, but Jack grabbed at his arm. 'You haven't done the thing with your fingers yet, Dad.' Matt shot her a questioning look and Beth avoided his gaze.

'Look, like this.' Jack tipped his father's face back towards him, laying one hand under his chin and carefully moving the other back and forth. He nodded slightly, in an almost flawless impression of what Beth had done, then suddenly made a face, hooting with laughter.

Embarrassment crawled across the back of her neck. Okay, so crossing her eyes and sticking out her tongue had made Jack laugh, but she wasn't so sure that his father would consider it particularly professional.

A deep chuckle shook his frame. 'All right. That does it.' He had his back turned to Beth, but from Jack's reaction it was apparent that Matt had risen to the challenge and was indulging in a face-pulling contest. Jack grimaced horribly and Matt rose. 'You win. No one with a face like that can have a great deal wrong with them.' He turned to Beth. 'Thank you. Do you know what's happening with his carer, Mrs Green?'

He spoke quietly, without exaggerating the movements of his mouth, and faced her. When most people heard her speak and divined from her accent that she was deaf, they looked away and shouted, neither of which helped in the slightest.

'I can hear you.' She'd rather say it upfront than leave people to wonder. He nodded but still his eyes never left her face. 'I called Phyllis to find out where you were and she's trying to locate Mrs Green. She'll call as soon as she knows.'

'Thanks. I really appreciate your kindness.' He perched himself on the edge of his desk, leaving Jack to play with the penlight. 'So you found him outside the hearing therapy unit? Is that where everyone who gets lost looking for Cardiology eventually ends up?'

So he did remember her. Beth couldn't suppress the smile that sprang to her lips. 'Pretty much. Parallel universes will do that kind of thing.'

His face broke into a wide grin. 'That they will.' The gleam in his eyes extinguished suddenly. 'And he was all on his own?'

'He must have given the staff the slip when the ambulance crew handed over to Casualty. He was looking for you.'

Matt let out a growl of exasperation. 'Jack, how many times have I told you—?'

Beth's phone came to Jack's rescue, vibrating suddenly in her pocket. 'This must be Phyllis.' She glanced at the caller display. 'Here. You'd better speak to her.' Phyllis had a knack of being able to speak in whole paragraphs before she needed to draw breath and Matt was more likely to be able to keep up with her on the phone.

He took the handset with a grin and pressed it against his ear. Barely getting a 'hello' in, he nodded and then a thumbs up in Beth's direction told her that Mrs Green was not too badly hurt.

'That's great, Phyllis, thanks. I'll take him

up there to see her… Can you call—? Great… thanks.' He snapped the phone shut and handed it back to Beth and then his attention was all for Jack, who had been fidgeting miserably in his seat. 'Rough day, eh, mate?'

Jack nodded, sliding down from the chair towards Matt, who lifted him effortlessly into his arms. 'Is Mrs Green really going be all right?' Jack's hands were clasped tightly around his father's neck and he seemed to be wiping his nose on Matt's shirt.

'Yes. She's hurt her wrist and her ribs are very sore, but they're looking after her very well right here in the hospital. She'll be as good as new before you know it.' He tipped Jack's face up towards his and Beth found herself smiling at the almost unbearable tenderness of the gesture. 'We can go and see her later and you'll be able to check her out for yourself. In the meantime, Phyllis is ringing your gran and she'll come and fetch you.'

Jack brightened visibly, wriggling in his father's grip, and Matt let him back down onto his feet. 'That's all right, Dad. I can stay with Beth.'

'No. Beth's got enough to do, without coming to our rescue every time you and I decide to get lost.' He flashed her a delicious grin. Warm and confiding, with a hint of mischief. Perfectly calculated. Beth reckoned he had his patients eating out of his hand with that one.

The phone on his desk rang and Matt snatched it up. From the way that he listened first, rather than talking, it was obviously Phyllis on the other end. 'Okay, thanks, Phyllis... No, I'll work something out... Yeah, thanks, I'll call you.' He laid the handset back in its cradle and focused on the stack of patient files on his desk, a muscle twitching at the side of his jaw.

'Childcare problems?' It seemed a bit presumptuous to ask, but Matt was clearly torn between his son and his patients.

'Yeah. I haven't quite mastered the knack of being in two places at once yet.'

'If you have patients to see then I can look after Jack. We have a children's play area in the HTU, and I don't have any appointments this afternoon. He'll be quite safe. Marcie and I won't let him out of our sight.'

It was an obvious solution, but for some reason Matt seemed intent on pursuing his original course of action. 'Thank you, that's kind, but I really can't impose on you like that. Phyllis has offered to take care of him in my office if she can't reach my mother.'

Jack tugged at his arm. 'That's all right, Dad. I'll go with Beth and you can come and fetch me later. The hearing place is much nicer than your office.'

'We've got paints. And glitter pens. We could make Mrs Green a get-well-soon card.' Beth winked conspiratorially at Jack, who shot his father a pleading look.

Matt hesitated. It seemed there was one person, at least, who had the power to veto his instructions. 'You're going to do exactly as Beth tells you, aren't you? Leave the messing around for tonight, when you get home.'

Jack's outraged expression made it plain that messing about had never been further from his thoughts and Matt laughed down at his son. 'Okay, then. Looks as if the lady with the glitter pens has outbid me.'

CHAPTER TWO

ALL afternoon, the grey eyes, which warmed to a colour he could not quite define when Beth smiled, had been beckoning to Matt and he had doggedly ignored the summons. Bitter experience had already taught him that distractions of this kind led to dangerous places. Anyway, no one had eyes that great, it must have been a trick of the light.

Slipping through the open door of the hearing therapy unit, he found himself in a small reception area, with a wide archway leading through to another room, which seemed to be set up as an informal association area. He could hear Jack's voice and went to walk towards it when something in the boy's tone made him stop.

'My mum was in a road accident like Mrs Green.' There was a silence and Matt started forward again, freezing again when he heard Jack continue.

'She wasn't all right, though. She died.'

There was a rustle, as if someone had moved in their seat, and he heard Beth's voice, clear and melodic. 'I would be very sad if that happened to me.'

Jack spoke again. 'Is that how you say you feel sad? With your hand like that?'

'Yes.' There was a pause. 'That's right, Jack, you are telling me that you feel sad.'

Matt sagged back against the wall, unprepared for the violence of the emotion that had hit him. Jack was talking about his mother at last. After two years of hardly even referring to her his silence had been broken. His lips twisted at the irony of it. Jack's silence had not been broken. He had found another way to express his feelings.

'My dad feels sad, too, but he doesn't say so.' Jealousy stabbed at Matt, twisting the knife in his chest. Why was Jack talking to a virtual stranger when his own father had tried so hard to be there for him?

'Sometimes when you feel sad, you try to hide that from the people you love the best.' Matt shook his head as the words reached him. She was absolutely right, but it was more complicated than that. But Jack was never to know that. No one was.

'It's because I'm just a kid.' There was a trace of resentment in Jack's voice.

'You're not *just* anything. And it's your dad's job to look after you, Jack.' Her tone invited no argument.

'I bet no one had to look after you when you were a kid.'

Beth laughed. 'Oh, yes, they did. Shall I tell you a secret?'

Perhaps he shouldn't listen. On the other hand, the kind of secret you told to a child was unlikely to be anything too earth-shattering. Matt found himself leaning forward.

'I've got a big brother called Charlie. When I was little, he could hear much better than I could, and I hated it when he tried to help me. It made me feel stupid, as if I couldn't do anything right. I used to pretend I could hear things when I couldn't.'

'How did you do that?'

'Oh, there are lots of ways you can tell what people are saying without hearing them. Even if you can't see their lips properly to read them, the expressions on their faces can tell you what they're thinking. You just have to look.'

Were his own secrets written on his face? Matt swallowed hard. Of course not, he was just being paranoid. Beth had made a connection with Jack, not him.

There was silence and then Beth spoke again. 'I'm sure you do miss your mum. But you don't need to finger-spell all the words. Look, you can say it like this.'

Matt squeezed his eyes shut. He would have given anything to hear Jack say the words that he knew were forming silently on his hands. But this would have to be enough for the moment. Beth had the tone exactly right—just a simple exercise in how to sign, which was allowing Jack to approach topics that he hadn't spoken about before. Why on earth hadn't he thought of something like that?

Dared he try to catch a glimpse of them? Standing here was torture, but he knew that it was important to give Jack time to say everything he wanted to.

'That's right.' Jack had obviously got the signs she had taught him correct. 'Now, I'll show you something else that you might want to say to your dad.'

'I know what that is!' Jack exclaimed excitedly, and there was silence again as he signed back to her.

'No—look, like this.'

Another pause, and her soft laugh sounded, curling around Matt's senses like a gentle summer breeze. 'Well done, you're very good at this.'

They had obviously concluded their business and Matt reckoned it was about time he got Jack home. He was going to have to wait to find out what it was that Beth had thought Jack might like to say to him, and the urge to see both of them was becoming irresistible. He stepped forward into the wide archway, as if he had just walked in through the door.

She caught sight of him, and for a moment all Matt could think about was that her eyes, still dancing with laughter, were even more compellingly beautiful than he had remembered. It wasn't just her eyes either. Every time he looked at her he seemed to find something else that fascinated him.

'Hello, there.' Her voice broke the spell, and Jack's head, just visible above the back of the chair facing her, bobbed as he scrambled round to see his father. 'We were just…' Her hands moved almost unconsciously and Matt wondered whether the words that had not escaped her lips were being formed by her fingers.

Jack ran to him, throwing his hands around his waist, and Matt dropped his case, his hands on his son's back, his eyes still imprisoned in the curve of her lips. Her hair was tied up in a messy bun, as if she had scraped it impatiently out of the way, little strands waving around her face in the kind of effect that a hairdresser might take hours to achieve. As she tilted her head towards him he caught sight of the cochlear implant that had been hidden by her hair the last time he had seen her.

It took a conscious effort to drag his gaze from her face and look down at Jack. 'Have you been good for Beth?' Even her name seemed to linger in his senses, brushing his lips like the promise of a kiss.

Jack nodded vigorously and Beth smiled at him. 'It's been a pleasure having him down here.' She looked at her watch. 'You're a little early.' The words were almost a reproach and her manner seemed slightly changed, a shade more distant than earlier on.

'Yeah. One of my patients didn't turn up for his appointment and a couple were early, so I'm ahead of schedule for once.'

She made no comment. Matt moved awkwardly into the room, hampered by the fact that Jack had slipped his fingers through his belt and was trying to tug him towards her. Suddenly, the way forward became blindingly obvious.

His fingers brushed her elbow and Beth almost yelped as she jumped back. She didn't want him touching her, not now. Not after the bombshell that Jack had just dropped. Somewhere, alongside the sorrow at a woman's death and the clawing regret that a child should have to suffer this, there had been sympathy for Matt. And however natural that might be, it was still an emotion. She didn't trust herself with any kind of emotion when it came to Matt Sutherland.

'I want to thank you for this afternoon. I really appreciate everything you've done for Jack.' He had reacted to her start and was maintaining a safe distance now.

'It's been my pleasure. Jack's been keeping me company and helping out with lots of different things.' Jack wasn't the problem. It was his father who was unsettling her.

Beth turned her back on both of them, on the pretext of collecting her coat and handbag. Now that Matt was out of range and out of sight, she could think more clearly and her hands unconsciously repeated the resolutions that the heat of his smile had reshaped into restrictions. Stand on your own two feet. No more dating.

When she looked around, Matt was already cajoling Jack into his coat, and she tucked the display boards that she was taking home under one arm and slung her handbag across her shoulder. Pausing to sign a goodbye to Jack, she made for the door.

Jack signed back to her and then turned to Matt. 'You don't know what I said to Beth, do you?'

'Not a clue, mate.' Matt gave her a conspiratorial wink that would have melted an iceberg. 'Care to tell me?'

Jack shook his head and turned to Beth. 'It's our secret language and my dad doesn't know what we're saying.'

The son was so like his father, blond and blue eyed, but so unlike him as well. Jack was lively and open, his thoughts and feelings easy to read.

'Not much of a secret around here, Jack. Every-one knows how to sign.'

'Yes, but my dad doesn't.' Jack flashed Matt a look of reproach.

'Well, perhaps you'll teach me, then.' Matt rumpled his son's hair, his easy warmth surfac-ing again.

'Beth could teach you.' Jack stretched up to-wards his father confidingly. 'Beth's got a bionic ear.'

Jack looked at her for approval and Beth grinned. One of the things she liked about chil-dren was their ability to refer to her cochlear implant as if it was something to be proud of.

'It's pretty neat, isn't it?' Matt sounded as im-pressed as Jack had been. 'All the same, I want *you* to teach me what you've learned today.' His jaw tightened and Beth wondered again whether he had heard any of her conversation with Jack.

Jack heaved a theatrical sigh and waited at Matt's side while Beth pulled her coat on and dumped the display boards outside the door, fish-ing in her handbag for her keys. Before she'd even slid the key into the lock, Matt had picked up the boards, tucking them under his arm along with his heavy-looking case. 'Let me carry these to your car.'

'No, that's okay. My car's in the garage, so I'm on the bus.' The way he'd picked her things up, without asking, had put her on edge. If she had needed any help she would have said so.

'In that case, let me give you a lift home. Where do you live?'

He gave her a 'don't argue' look and Beth wondered how many people in Matt's life contested his decisions. Probably not that many. 'Easington. The bus goes from the hospital grounds practically to my door.'

'And we go past Easington and can drop you off right at your door. Jack, pick Beth's gloves up and bring them along.' Beth looked down to where her gloves lay on the floor, realising that she must have dropped them out of her coat pocket. Before she could retrieve them, Jack had pounced on them and was rolling them up in the end of his father's dark blue scarf.

She might have had few scruples about arguing with Matt, however lofty his position, but Jack was a different matter. From the smug look on Matt's face he had obviously been banking on that very fact and was pleased to have been proved right. Beth swallowed her reservations, locked the doors of the hearing therapy unit and followed the two of them to the staff car park.

It was already dark and sleet was bouncing off the windscreen of the car. Out of the shelter of the city, the roads were thick with ice and Beth began to be thankful that she wasn't waiting at a windy bus stop or sitting on a bus as it wound its way around all the neighbouring villages before finally reaching her own.

She'd be home soon. Safe and sound in the protective cocoon she'd made for herself after Pete had left. And Matt Sutherland would be driving away, taking his disturbing smile with him, along with all the reactions it provoked in her.

Without thinking, she brushed his arm to get his attention. The gesture, so automatic among the deaf, seemed suddenly too intimate and she snatched her hand away. 'Turn left here. There's a row of cottages a little way down. Mine's the one at the far end.'

She was scrabbling for the doorhandle almost as soon as he drew up. He turned the engine off with a decisive motion and went to get out of the car. 'Stay put, Jack, I've just got to talk to Beth for a moment.'

What now? She shivered impatiently in the cold night air as Matt retrieved her display boards from the boot, propping them up against the wheel arch instead of giving them straight to her.

'Jack doesn't talk much about his mother,' he started stiffly. 'I heard you talking with him and wanted to thank you.'

So he *had* heard. Beth licked her lips nervously. 'I didn't mean to pry into your business.'

'You didn't. Jack has every right to say whatever he likes to whoever he likes, he doesn't need my permission. He doesn't do it enough.'

'I'm glad he felt he could talk about her today, then. I really did enjoy spending the afternoon with him, he's a great kid.'

He nodded. 'I…I hope we'll see you again. It would be nice if you could join us for lunch some time. As a thank you. You've given him a way to express his feelings, and I'm truly grateful for that.' She was pretty sure he had that engaging smile on his face again. Out here in the darkness it was difficult to tell.

'Sometimes things that can't be said one way can be said in another.' Beth ignored Matt's invitation and concentrated on Jack. 'I've got some wall charts that show the finger-spelling alphabet and some simple signs. If he'd like one, I can drop it in to Phyllis next week some time.' That seemed safe enough.

His voice warmed with enthusiasm. 'Thank you, I'd really appreciate that. It won't do him any harm to learn another language and…' He was suddenly lost for words.

'I know. Anything that gives him a voice. I understand, I used to do the same thing myself when I was little. All my secrets were signed.' Apart from the one she'd told Jack. Beth flushed. If he'd heard that then no wonder he hadn't taken her refusal of his offer of a lift too seriously.

He grinned and then the smile slid from his face. He was looking intently over her shoulder and Beth turned to face her cottage.

'Do you leave a light on when you're out?'

Through the front window she could see a light, glimmering unsteadily inside the house. As she strained to see where it was coming from the porch light flickered on and back off again as if it was trying to signal something. Her hand flew to her mouth as she caught her breath.

'Obviously not. Give me your keys, I'll go and take a look. It's probably an electrical fault of some sort.'

'Thanks, but I think I can manage to avoid sticking my fingers into any dodgy light sockets. I can handle it.'

'I dare say you can. But if someone's broken in and they're still there you're not handling that alone. I'll just go and make sure.'

'Perhaps—'

He gave a little huff of impatience. 'Perhaps nothing. Here.' He grabbed her hand and put his keys into it. 'Stay in the car and if I'm not back in five, you drive to the nearest police station. Please—someone needs to look after Jack.'

His final words were tacked on almost as an afterthought, but the command in his tone had slipped away. Beth followed his gaze to the back seat of the car where Jack was twisting around fretfully, trying to get out of his seat belt.

She pulled her keys out of her bag and pushed them into his hand, before getting into the driver's seat of the car. Matt shut the door behind her, indicating with his thumb that she should lock the doors, before turning and heading up her front path.

CHAPTER THREE

SHE shouldn't have let him go. Now that she was alone here in the car with Jack, there wasn't much she could do about it, though. She kept up a steady stream of conversation with Jack, at the same time straining to see as Matt swept the beam of the torch over the front door and the windows, looking for signs of forced entry before letting himself in. The torch beam flicked back and forth in the hallway, then in her tiny front room and then disappeared.

What if there was someone in there? What if they hurt him? Matt was tall and imposing but if there was more than one intruder they might get the better of him. She squinted at her watch in the darkness. Had he really only been gone for three minutes?

Tears of relief pricked at the side of her eyes as she saw him hurry down the front path. Motioning to her to unlock the car doors, he slid into the passenger seat. 'Looks as if you have a burst pipe. Do you know where the stopcock is? And the fusebox?' He gestured back at the porch, where the light was still flickering on and off. 'If that light is anything to go by, the water's got into the electrics.'

Of course she knew where they were—what did he take her for? Beth bit back her annoyance and remembered that just a few seconds ago she had been glad to see him emerge from the cottage in one piece. 'Under the stairs, in a little cupboard. Both the stopcock and the fusebox.'

He got out of the car without a word and was on his way back up the front path before she had the opportunity to tell him that she was perfectly capable of turning the water off and mopping up a few spills.

Matt let himself back into the cottage and dodged the curtain of water falling down the stairwell. His feet squelched on the hall carpet and by the light of the torch he could see that the wallpaper was beginning to peel. Finding the hall cupboard, he twisted the stopcock and flipped the mains electrical switch to off. Then he opened a door at the end of the hallway, figuring correctly that it led to the kitchen, and made for the sink. Turning both taps on, he let the water run, hoping that the water tank in the loft would drain quickly.

He knew that the longer he stayed there, the more Beth would be worrying and that he should get back to her. He didn't want her to have to see the cascade of water that had greeted him when he first entered, though. The place was enough of a mess, without that. Matt heard a gurgle as the tank finally drained and turned off the kitchen taps as the water coming through the ceiling slowed to a steady dribble.

He trudged back to the car and knocked on the window. She turned, a brittle smile on her face, and the electric window whirred downwards. 'Can I help you?'

She was tough. Not many people would have even attempted a joke in this situation. The reassuring smile that Matt had pasted onto his face warmed as respect washed through him. 'Yeah. I was wondering if you might like to swap that six-year-old you have there for a cottage. It's a little wet at the moment, but it's basically sound.'

She pretended to think about it for a moment. 'Okay, you've got a deal.' The central locking on the car sounded and she climbed out, waiting while Matt unbuckled Jack's seat belt and chivvied him out of his booster seat.

He had half expected her to run straight into the house, but she was standing stock still, searching his face in the dim light. 'It's not...' Matt shrugged and handed her the flashlight. 'You'll be wanting to see for yourself, won't you?'

'Yes. Thanks.' Her smile was beginning to wear a little thin at the edges, and he caught her cold hand in his and led her up the front path.

Beth stood in the hallway, cold water creeping into her shoes, and watched as a piece of the wallpaper she had hung so carefully just a few weeks ago peeled slowly off the wall and landed on the carpet in a sodden mass. *Smile.* The words of the old song that her grandmother used to sign with her echoed in her head and she gave it her best shot.

'Perhaps that wallpaper was a bit much for a small hallway.'

Matt tilted his head to one side thoughtfully. 'Yeah. Perhaps.' He'd picked Jack up so that his feet didn't get wet, and had him safe and secure in his arms.

'At least I've got the hang of it now. Putting something else up will be easy. And the insurance will cover it.' She was babbling, trying to make out that everything was okay when it wasn't. She went to sit down on the stairs, and then jumped back to her feet as she realised the stair carpet was as wet as everything else.

'It's more than just the money, though, isn't it?' His quiet comment cut through all her pretence of being able to cope with this.

'Yes. I've only been here for eight months. It was…it *is* the first time I've had a place of my own. I did everything myself.' It had almost been a point of honour. Beth had wanted to show everyone, herself included, that she could manage her life on her own terms after Pete had left her.

'Then I'll bet you've already done plenty of things that seemed impossible at first. The initial shock is always the worst.'

Was he really so sure about that? 'I could kick myself. You know, I've never even been up in the loft to look at the water tank or the pipes. The surveyor said they were okay and I just took his word for it. Maybe if I'd….' She tailed off before her tears choked her. It was already too late to mend the damage that had been done to her dream. Everyone who had ever said that she couldn't fend for herself had just been proved right. And she'd proved it with her own stupid negligence.

'It's not your fault.' His tone was gentle but firm. How did someone get to be that sure about life?

The belief that she could cope with whatever life threw at her had just been unceremoniously ripped away, leaving her naked and shivery. And even though he was saying all the right things, Matt's solid dependability wasn't helping. The temptation to look as pathetic as she felt and cling to him was too much to bear.

Beth straightened herself, ignoring the hand-stands her stomach was doing, and swung the torch beam up from the carpet, trying to inspect the damage calmly. 'I *can* do this.'

'Yes, you can. It's a bit of a mess right now, but this is the worst of it. The water's off now and I've drained the tank.'

Thanks for reminding me. It was Matt who'd had the presence of mind to do that straight away, not her. Beth turned away from him, wiping her face with the sleeve of her coat.

'The back room isn't so bad,' he continued. 'It's worst in the hall and the sitting room.'

Beth nodded, trying not to start crying again

and feeling the tears trickle down her cheek anyway. What the hell—a few tears weren't going to make this place any wetter.

'Come and take a look.' He took her hand, holding it tight, and guided her to the small dining room, which lay behind the sitting room. She could see a few dribbles of water running down the walls but the carpet was dry to her touch and the furniture looked undamaged.

This wasn't so bad. 'Thank you for helping out. I'll be okay now.' She wanted him to go before his reassurance became completely indispensable. Then she could inspect the damage, have a good cry and work out what she was going to do next.

'No, you won't.' Jack lay motionless against his shoulder, obviously tired and bored. 'You'll freeze in this weather with no heating and in a wet house. If you want to stay with a friend then I'll take you wherever you need to go, but I live five miles down the road and I have a spare bedroom that's warm and dry. Come and stay with us tonight. There's nothing more that we can do until tomorrow.'

Beth stared at him. Warm and dry sounded like heaven at the moment, but she couldn't. She would rather be here, however uncomfortable it was. 'I'm fine, really.'

Matt gave a little gesture of impatience, and Jack stirred in his arms. 'No, you're not fine. And you most certainly won't be fine tomorrow if you spend the night here.' He gestured up and to the front of the house. 'If your bedroom's above the sitting room, then it's going to be wet through. It's already below freezing outside and you've no heating.'

Cold disappointment dripped into Beth's heart. He was right, of course, but she still didn't want to admit that she was reliant on the hospitality of a virtual stranger. She stared at Matt, unable to think of anything to say that sounded even vaguely rational.

'Are there any friends or family close by that you can call?'

Beth shook her head. 'On any other evening I'd call Marcie. But it's her wedding anniversary tonight and she's been planning it for weeks. And my parents are away in America, visiting my younger brother.' She could probably make it down to Charlie's place in London before midnight, but if she did he'd still be reminding her about this in thirty years' time.

'So come back to our place. The hospital's vetted me, so the chances of me not being an axe murderer are pretty much in your favour.' The veneer slipped and an irresistible grin broke through. 'And my son will vouch for me.' Jack was dozing fitfully now and didn't seem disposed to vouch for anyone at the moment. 'When he wakes up, that is.'

Beth's resolve wavered. The heat of Matt's smile was about the only thing around here that was much above freezing. 'I don't suppose that anywhere I want to go includes a hotel, does it? There's one a few miles down the road.'

'Right in one. No hotels.'

If she was going to take him up on his offer, she may as well do it gracefully. Beth smiled up at him and saw a glimmer in his dark blue eyes that looked suspiciously like triumph. 'Then your spare bedroom sounds like a lifesaver. It's very kind of you, thank you.'

Matt had left Jack curled up in a chair in the dining room while he had helped her wipe the puddles from the few good pieces of furniture she had and prop them up off the soaked carpets. The sofa cushions had been arranged on their ends around the sitting room so they could drain a little and he had rolled up the old rug, which was completely beyond saving, and dumped it in the back garden.

She had drawn the line at letting him into her bedroom but after seeing the waterlogged state of her bed had reluctantly called him to help her tip the mattress on one side against the wall. They had gathered up her soaking quilt and some of her clothes and put them into plastic bags in the boot of Matt's car and Beth had picked up her photo albums and her jewellery box and tucked them away on the back seat. Almost as an after-thought she had fetched her laptop, which seemed to have survived the deluge, and had found that Matt had picked up her textphone and was care-fully wiping it dry.

With one load of clothes in the washing ma-chine and another in the dryer, Beth finally al-lowed herself to relax into the sofa in front of the open fire at Matt's, watching the logs sizzle and spit as heat drove the moisture from them. Jack had claimed a place next to her and Matt had prepared soup with French bread for them all.

'That was nice. Must be home-made, it's got chunky bits.'

'My mother makes it. My parents live close by and she delivers it by the gallon and puts it in the freezer.' Matt was sitting on an easy chair, drawn up by the fire, inspecting her textphone. He had changed into jeans and a sweater and his short fair hair was dishevelled from where he had been running his hand through it, making him look even more like a grown-up version of the child that was currently dozing in her arms.

Beth tried not to look at his hands as his long fingers set to work, teasing the back off her phone. Capable hands, which looked as if they could be as gentle as they were precise. He wore no wedding ring and she wondered whether he had done once.

'So you grew up around here?'

'Yes. You?'

'London.' Beth tucked her legs under her on the sofa, letting Jack slide into her lap, feeling herself relax in the heat from the fire. 'My family's pretty scattered now, though. My parents moved down to the South Coast when Dad retired and my younger brother's in the States. He's a member of a Deaf Theatre Company over there.'

'Sounds interesting. What does he do?'

'He's an actor. They're based in New York but

they take their productions all over the country. He loves it.'

'The pull of an audience can be very seductive.' There was an edge to Matt's voice.

'Oh, Nathan's got his priorities right. He's just married a really nice girl—she keeps him grounded.'

'Smart guy.' The bitterness in Matt's tone was unmistakable now and he changed the subject quickly. 'Are your parents deaf as well?'

'My father is. Mum's hearing.' Beth took a deep breath. She may as well say it. She was proud of who she was and was damned if she was going to hide it as if it were some kind of embarrassing secret. 'I have autosomal dominant deafness. That means…'

He silenced her with an amused look. 'I know. One dominant gene, inherited from your father, and not a recessive gene inherited from each parent.'

Of course he knew. Genetics 101. 'Yes. Mum and Dad knew pretty much what to expect when they had children. With the dominant gene there was always going to be a fifty-fifty chance of each of us being deaf.' Her throat constricted suddenly as if she was being choked.

'But your mother saw past that.'

'Yeah. Just as well for me and my brothers.' Pete hadn't. Neither had his mother, who had already persuaded him that he was perfect and didn't have much difficulty convincing him that his children should be, too.

Beth looked down at the child dozing in her lap. She was surrounded by all the things that Pete had promised her and then reneged on. All the things she had sworn she wouldn't think about any more. She began to feel sick again.

'Are you okay?' Beth focused back on Matt with an effort of will and saw concern in his face. 'You look very pale.'

'Yes, fine.'

'Sure you don't feel dizzy? Or hot and cold?'

'No. Neither.' The room had stopped lurching now, and the heat from the fire was warming her again.

'Nausea?'

'No.' The feeling had passed and Matt's obvious frustration at her lack of symptoms was making her feel much better.

'May I take your pulse?'

'I'll do it.' Beth wasn't sure if her heart really did beat twice as fast whenever he touched her but she wasn't taking any chances. She counted off the beats against the second hand of the clock on the mantelpiece. 'Dead on sixty.'

'Hmm. Very good. Excellent, in fact. Would you like a cup of tea?'

'I'm not in shock.'

'You probably are, very slightly. Anyone would be after tonight.' He sighed and gave up. 'I suppose there's no harm in offering you a non-medicinal drop of brandy.'

Beth giggled. The way this man could take her from the depths of depression back to laughter in a matter of minutes was frightening. 'That sounds more like it. Thanks, just a splash.'

He rose and opened the glass door of a cabinet fitted in the alcove beside the chimney breast, withdrawing two cut-glass tumblers and a brandy bottle. Pouring a couple of mouthfuls into each, he placed one next to her and returned to his seat with the other. Jack stirred, reaching out for her, and Beth coiled her arm back around him. Tipping her glass towards Matt in a silent toast, she took a sip of the brandy and settled back against the cushions. Crisis over.

It made Matt smile, seeing the two of them like this on the sofa, Jack curled up in Beth's arms, sleeping peacefully. Her eyes were luminous in the firelight and she looked even smaller, even more fine-boned in the rolled-up jogging pants and sweatshirt he had lent her.

He picked up the textphone, which lay beside his chair, and finally managed to prise the cover free. Water dribbled out over his jeans and he brushed it away, sending the drops fizzing into the fire.

Looking up, he realised that she had been watching him and heat started to build in his chest. The thought of her eyes on his hands, his lips, became almost too much to bear and he smiled awkwardly.

'We'll leave this open to dry out overnight and try it in the morning. It should be all right.' It seemed so natural to say *we* and he liked the fact that she gave the slightest of nods in response, as if she, too, accepted that for tonight at least they were a single unit. For the moment, anyway, she seemed to have abandoned her stubborn independence, melting into the small family by the fireside, somehow making both him and Jack whole again.

She was sipping the small portion of brandy he had allowed her, watching as he laid the phone out to dry by the hearth. 'So how's Jack settling in?'

'It's early days but he seems to be doing well. He loves being near my parents and his new school is great. I think it's made a big difference, getting away from the old house. He sleeps a lot better now.'

'That's good. A decent night's sleep always helps you face the day.'

'Yeah. I used to get up in the middle of the night and find him sitting downstairs, waiting for his mother to come home.' Matt pressed his lips together. Jack had done that regularly before his mother had died, as well as after.

Her fingers tightened around Jack's shoulders, as if she wanted to pull him close and hug him but was afraid of waking him. 'Well, he seems to be ready to talk a little about how he feels. It was a privilege to be there this afternoon.'

'I'm thankful that you were.' Matt could see why Jack had opened up to Beth. It was hard not to. But there were things he would never tell anyone, not even if Beth taught him the signs for them.

'Jack said his mother died in a car accident. I'm sorry I didn't realise that when I brought him down to see you this afternoon. It must have been a shock to hear that he'd almost been knocked down.' She twisted her fingers together.

Matt's heart felt as if it was actually melting. The sensation was an odd one and not entirely pleasant. 'Thank you, but it's okay.' He spread his hands in a gesture of reassurance. 'He was there with you and I could see he was all right. And my wife wasn't knocked down by a car. She'd been working away from home for a week and was driving back to London on the Friday evening when her car skidded on a patch of ice on the motorway.'

Beth's hand flew to her mouth. 'I'm so sorry. That she never got home.'

She hadn't been on her way home. She'd been on her way to a hotel, with her lover. Matt swallowed the truth, but couldn't bring himself to offer up the usual lie. 'Thank you.' He opted for a brisk change of subject. 'It's getting late. I'd better get this little guy up to bed.' He rose and lifted the sleeping boy out of Beth's arms, briefly scenting her hair before he managed to put some space between them again.

Jack stirred and rubbed his eyes. 'Story, Dad.'

'You bet. Let's get you upstairs and we'll have a story there.'

'Why not down here?' Matt knew what Jack was angling for. He wanted Beth to tell him a story.

'No, mate.' He retrieved the copy of *Robin Hood and his Merrie Men* from where Jack had dumped it that morning and tucked it against his chest. 'Beth probably doesn't like Robin Hood.'

He could see from her face that she wouldn't have minded reading Jack's bedtime story one little bit. He minded, though. Having Beth read to Jack, when his mother had made so little effort to be home in time to do so, would have been like rubbing salt into open wounds.

'Okay. Just you and me, Dad. The two musketeers.' Jack snuggled into his chest and the familiar, overpowering need to protect him surged through Matt. He couldn't risk the possibility of his son going through the pain of abandonment for a second time. He couldn't take the risk for himself either. As far as Beth was concerned, friendship wasn't just the best option, it was the only option.

Regret hung in the air for a brief moment, before dispersing under the relentless pressure of his resolve. As if to prove to himself that he could do it, Matt wrenched his gaze away from Beth and then turned, making for the stairs.

CHAPTER FOUR

LEFT alone, Beth collected the mugs and plates from the table by the fire and took them into the kitchen, washing them and putting them away. Walking back into the sitting room, she realised what had seemed odd to her about the place. It was comfortable, practical and quietly stylish but all the furniture seemed new and everything was arranged just so. Apart from a mess of toys and books to one side of the hearth, there were none of the quirky, out-of-place bits and pieces that were collected over time, and which made her own cottage seem like a home.

Almost the only personal things in the room were a group of picture frames grouped on the dresser, and Beth paused to look at them. Matt and Jack. Matt with an older man and woman, and a young woman who was so like him she had to be his sister. She picked up a third picture, one of Jack with a different woman, his arms flung around her neck. The woman was dark, well groomed and looked into the camera with a self-possessed smile that seemed vaguely familiar.

This must be Matt's wife. The woman who ought to be here with him and Jack, while Beth should be at home, where she belonged. Her fingers trembled as she went to replace the photograph and she started guiltily to find Matt standing beside her.

'Oh. I'm sorry.' Once again he had surprised her snooping.

Matt shrugged. 'What for?' He picked up the photo and looked at it thoughtfully. 'That's Jack's mother, Mariska.'

Mariska Sutherland. The name rang a bell, too. 'She was very beautiful.' She wished that she was not wearing clothes that were at least four sizes too big and feeling unbearably dowdy in comparison.

Matt nodded absently. 'She was a journalist, and she travelled a lot for her work.' It was like a well-rehearsed answer to a question she hadn't even asked.

Beth remembered now. 'I've seen her show. I don't usually catch daytime TV but I recorded the programme she did on cochlear implants. I thought it was very good—very clear and even-handed.' All of the air seemed to have been sucked out of the room and she was struggling to breathe, let alone find the right words to say. 'It must have been a terrible shock to lose her so suddenly.'

Matt gave her an odd look that she couldn't quite fathom. 'Yeah. Although she was away from home a lot. In many ways Jack and I were used to being on our own.' He fixed his eyes on the floor, studying it intently. 'He went to sleep straight away tonight, though. Stayed awake long enough to ask if you'd be here in the morning and then he was out like a light. I didn't even get as far as Robin Hood.'

Beth grinned. 'I don't have anywhere else to go. Not till tomorrow, anyway.'

He nodded and for a moment their eyes locked. She felt as if she was falling towards him, into him, stopping only to brush the softness of his lips. Beth broke free with an effort and took a step back from him.

He made no indication of having noticed. 'It's been a tough day for all of us. I'm ready to drop.

Make yourself at home here and sleep well, I'll see you in the morning.'

He turned abruptly, not waiting for her answer, and made for the fireplace, raking over the ashes to make sure that they were properly extinguished and closing the damper to conserve the heat in the room. He paused only to issue a curt 'Goodnight' in Beth's direction and then he was gone.

Mariska's portrait drew her attention back over to the sideboard. She'd been accomplished, beautiful and successful. This was the kind of woman that someone like Matt could love—that he had loved. If Beth had needed any proof that her reaction to Matt's smile and the brush of his fingers was strictly one-sided, then here it was.

A stab of regret gave way to a grin. Could she be any more perverse if she tried? One minute she was willing Matt to be out of reach and the next she was regretting the fact that he was. Beth rolled her eyes at her own foolishness, collected her handbag and padded up the stairs to the room that was to be hers for the night.

It appeared that father and son were working as a team the following morning. As Jack helped Beth fold her clean clothes into a pile, ready to take back with her, Matt disappeared into the garage, reappearing again with a workmanlike toolbox and a length of copper pipe, which he loaded into the boot of his car along with the rest of her possessions.

From the way that they were both dressed, jeans, heavy jumpers and in Matt's case a pair of thick-soled boots, it looked unlikely that he intended to simply drop her off at her cottage. As Matt produced a pair of red Wellingtons and a second pair of socks, insisting that Jack put them on, Beth wondered what he was intending to do with his morning, and when he intended to inform her about it.

Her cottage looked deceptively cheery from the outside, but inside it was a very different matter. The place was already beginning to smell damp and everything was cold and wet, including the walls. Matt dumped his toolbox in the hall and peered up the stairs at the loft hatch. 'I'll just go and take a look in the loft. Have you got a ladder?'

'Please, you've done enough already. I texted Marcie this morning and she and her husband should be here in a couple of hours.'

He gave her a hurt look. 'I'm pretty handy with

a wrench. Learned all I know from my father—he's a plumber and electrician by trade and has his own contracting company. He was very upset when I failed to follow in his footsteps and went to medical school.'

Matt's lopsided grin gave the lie to any disappointment on his father's part. A vision of what else Matt might be handy with flew into her head and she turned to Jack, trying to ignore the heat that was spreading through her. 'Is there any end to your dad's talents?'

'Well, as Jack points out, I'm pretty deficient when it comes to signing. So I'll just leave you two down here to send a few secret messages to each other while you're mopping up.' He gave her a wink, and suddenly he became an essential part of the rest of her morning.

Jack stamped on the wet carpet, his Wellington boots throwing up little splashes of water, and Beth couldn't help but laugh. 'I guess I don't have much choice.'

'No, you don't. Jack, find the torch for me, will you?'

By the time Matt reappeared from the loft, an hour later, Beth was wiping the kitchen cupboards dry and Jack was tipping water from cups and bowls into the sink. His jeans were grimy from the loft and a streak of dirt ran across his brow, where he had obviously swept his hand across it. He looked about ten years younger and a world away from the tightly buttoned man that she had met yesterday.

'Will you turn the water on if I shout when I'm ready?' He took the stairs two at a time when she nodded her assent, and she craned to watch him disappear up through the loft hatch on the upstairs landing.

Matt's 'Okay' came booming down the stairs and Beth twisted the stopcock, hearing the pipes gurgle and bang as water rushed through them. She held her breath, waiting for any signs of a leak. Jack capered at the bottom of the stairs and turned to her as she strained to hear Matt's muffled voice.

'Dad says that it's all okay up there.' Jack skipped over to her and flung his arms round her neck and Beth stood up, lifting Jack with her and swinging him around. Suddenly her little house was hers again. The unruly cascades of water were back under control and she could start to think about cleaning up properly. After the shock of last night, when it had felt as if her whole world was crumbling around her, this was a huge step.

Matt appeared, grinning at his success, and before she knew what she was doing, Beth had laid her free hand on his shoulder and stood on her toes to brush a brief kiss across his cheek. Remembering herself, she drew back suddenly and found that Matt's hand had snaked around her, his palm on the small of her back. As quickly as she felt it there, he pulled away, almost as if she had burned him, and he took a step back.

'Water's back on.' He was grinning sheepishly.

Beth pulled at the sleeve of her jumper, feeling as self-conscious as Matt looked. 'Thank you.'

Now that a couple of feet separated them, he was more at ease. 'A pleasure, ma'am. Now, lets see how much water has got into the electrics. If I can isolate the circuit for the heating, it would be good to get that working at least.'

Beth's phone vibrated and she hastily put another couple of yards between her and Matt as she looked at the screen. Marcie had got her text from this morning and was on her way over with James and double-strength cappuccinos to inspect the damage.

Matt was tinkering with the light switches,

opening them up and allowing the water to drain out of them, when Beth saw the silver SUV manoeuvre along the lane and draw up behind Matt's Mercedes. Before Marcie or James had the opportunity to get out of the vehicle, she was jogging down the front path towards them.

Fortunately, little seemed to be able to penetrate their shared glow of good humour this morning. Beth's sleeping arrangements last night and Matt's presence here now were accepted without comment from Marcie and with an observation from James that he was glad she hadn't been trying to deal with this all on her own.

Marcie plucked two of the cardboard cups from the holder on her lap and handed them through the open window with a grin. Since Beth had already been rescued and it was unlikely that any further rescuing was going to be needed for the next hour, they would go and fetch Josh and Anna straight away.

When Beth let herself back into the house, Matt was in the hallway, looking as if he might be doing something. 'Was that Marcie?'

'Yes, and James, her husband. Here, they brought coffee.' She handed him one of the cups. 'There's sugar in the kitchen if you want it.'

'No, this is fine, thanks.' He wound his fingers around the tall cardboard cup, and Beth saw that they were red from the cold. He'd been working without gloves and although his down jacket was thick enough to keep him warm, his hands must be freezing.

'They're just going to pick the children up from Marcie's parents, and then they'll come back here. James said they'll stop off and hire a couple of those industrial blow heaters on the way. They'll be back in an hour.'

'Great. Well, I should be able to isolate the power circuits from the lighting ones by then, and we'll be able to get some heat in here.' He seemed in no mood to hurry away. Pleasure at the reprieve sneaked up and stabbed Beth in the back, like a treacherous lover.

However much she wanted to, though, she couldn't keep him there. 'Look, you've already done too much. It's not that I'm not grateful, Matt, but you must have a whole load of things to do. I'm okay, really.'

His eyes wandered around the wet hallway. 'Yeah, I can see that.' He lifted the lid of the cardboard cup and took a mouthful of the hot coffee. 'Let's just get on here. I'd be happier if we got the electricity back on. What do you think, Jack?' He glanced down at Jack, who had been standing between them, following the conversation.

'Yeah. We can't leave you on your own. You need our help.' Jack was obviously repeating his father's words to her and they stung like crazy. Did she really appear that pathetic? Beth laid her coffee cup down on the hall table, and bent down to face him.

'But it's really cold here, Jack. Aren't you getting cold?' She pulled off his glove and felt his hand. It was as warm as toast.

'No.' There was obvious solidarity between father and son on this point.

'And we're new in town here, remember? We're not exactly overwhelmed with places to go and people to see yet,' Matt broke in.

'In that case.... Well, if you'd really like to stay on and meet Marcie and James, that would be great. Marcie was going to take her two home for lunch and then to the cinema this afternoon to let James and I get on here. Perhaps Jack would like to go along with them.'

Matt looked at Jack for confirmation. 'Would you like to go to the cinema with Marcie? I'll

stay here with Beth and pick you up afterwards.'
He might be perfectly capable of steam-rollering
over Beth's wishes, but at least he listened to
those of his six-year-old.

'Yeah, Dad.' Jack was practically running on
the spot in a little dance of excitement. 'Is it the
film about the fishes? Marcie and I drew some
fishes on Mrs Green's card yesterday.'

Beth nodded. 'That's the one. Afterwards, perhaps you and your dad will come with us for
something to eat.' Matt drew a breath to speak
and Beth cut him short before he could say no.
'There's a new Italian restaurant in town. Meant
to be very good and it's family friendly.'

'Well…'

'I insist. My shout. It's the least I can do. Josh
and Anna are around Jack's age, so we won't be
making a late night of it.'

'I'm—'

'Go on, Dad!' Jack was tugging at his jacket.
'We never go anywhere.' Now Matt was on the
end of Jack's propensity to reveal the uncomfortable. He had clearly not been exaggerating when
he had indicated that their social life wasn't exactly glittering at the moment.

Matt held up his hands, laughing. 'Hold on a

minute!' Beth wasn't sure whether the instruction extended to her or not, but she fell silent anyway.

'Thank you—yes, we'd love to come.' He raised one eyebrow at Jack, who was too pleased with the acceptance to notice. Matt's grin became broader and Beth took Jack's lead and ignored him.

'Good. In that case I'll just be getting on with something.' Anything to conceal her flustered delight. She took Jack's hand and led him into the kitchen, wondering what on earth she had just let herself in for.

CHAPTER FIVE

IT HAD taken Matt a good four days to convince himself that the long, sociable Saturday evening, spent at a great little Italian restaurant and then back at Marcie and James's house for coffee, had been nothing other than a pleasant evening with new friends. Almost as soon as he had begun to relax in the comforting certainty of that illusion, Beth shattered it with one blow.

'Oh!' She had been walking at speed when she cannoned into him and as she staggered back from the impact, Matt's hand automatically shot out to steady her. 'Sorry!'

'Nothing broken.' Matt lied. The sudden warmth of her body against his had taken him unawares and crushed every one of his carefully constructed defences. Friendship wasn't all he wanted from her, not by any stretch of the imagination. 'Where are you going in such a hurry?'

'A and E.' She didn't stop and Matt fell into step

beside her. 'I got a call to say that a deaf couple are down there and can I help.'

'That's where I'm going. How come you're here this late?' Matt had to lengthen his stride slightly to keep up with her.

'We have a tinnitus club every other Thursday. Well, support group actually, but we like to think of it as more like a club, it allows us to bring along a few bottles and something to eat. So what about you? I didn't know the head of cardiology spent his evenings on call.' She was teasing him gently, and a faint tingle crawled up his spine.

'I don't. I am, however, allowed to answer the phone when it rings. Sometimes they even let me make a call or two.'

Beth grinned at him, her grey eyes dancing, and he felt his chest tighten. 'What will they come up with next? Are you going to see an angina case?'

'As it happens. Do you know something I don't or was that just a lucky guess?'

She rounded the corner and made for the doors to the A and E department. 'Your patient's name is Doug Grant and he's there with his wife, Jean. They're both deaf.'

'You know them?' The name rang a bell but

Matt couldn't quite place it. Well, surely there were many Doug Grants…

'Yeah. Jean asked the A and E staff to contact me.'

'That's a good start, then. Do they use speech or signing for preference?'

'Jean uses mainly signing. Doug has more hearing than her and can usually get by with hearing aids, but if he's not in good shape and needs to be lying down then he probably won't be wearing them. He'll be relying pretty heavily on Jean.'

'In that case, I'll be relying on you.' Matt wondered briefly why no one had thought to mention this when they had called him down and was glad that Beth was there. Moving quickly, he reached the swing doors before her, holding one open and letting her lead the way.

A brief exchange of wordless signals between her and the A and E receptionist were enough for her to locate the correct treatment booth, and Matt followed her inside. A middle-aged couple was alone in there, the man lying on a bed and the woman sitting beside him, holding his hand. The man was hooked up to an ECG machine, and Matt noticed a dressing on his arm, which indicated that blood had already been taken.

The woman brightened visibly when she saw Beth. A rapid succession of signs passed between them, and Matt waited for them to finish. Jean obviously had something to say, and it was important that someone take notice of that. Beth was nodding, and Matt positioned himself beside her, so that the woman could see his face.

Beth flashed him a look of approval. 'This is Jean and her husband Doug.' She was both signing and speaking, so that everyone in the booth could follow her. 'Doug had a bad angina attack this evening and the paramedics brought them in here. The doctor has taken blood, but beyond that they don't know what's going on and they're both very worried.' She gestured towards Matt. 'Jean, this is Dr Matt Sutherland. He is a cardiac specialist.'

Matt held his hand out to Jean, and she took it, smiling at him through the stress lines that were etched into her face. 'Tell them…' Matt thought better of his words and turned to Jean, speaking slowly and as clearly as he could. 'I'm going to assess your husband's ECG results.' He paused and indicated the machine that was monitoring Doug's heartbeat. 'And speak to the doctor who has already seen you. Then I will examine Doug and I may recommend that he stays in the hospital for tonight.'

A quick nod told him that Jean understood, and she signed to her husband. Matt waited for her to finish and turn her attention back to him. It was not usual practice to use a relative as an interpreter, but Matt also knew the value of communicating directly with patients and their families. Beth was there, keeping a close eye on him, and would make sure that nothing was missed.

'Has Doug had any aspirin? Any other medication? Either here or at home?'

Jean signed and then shrugged tearfully. Reaching into her handbag, she withdrew two bottles of tablets and pressed them into Matt's hand.

He looked quickly at the labels. Standard prescriptions for angina. 'Good. That's helpful, Jean, thank you.' He turned to Beth. 'What did she sign?'

'He's just had his regular medication.' Beth pointed to the tablets in his hand. 'She doesn't think they gave him anything else here but she's not absolutely sure. Do you want me to go and find the doctor who saw them?'

Matt nodded. She was here to interpret, not run errands, but at this point clinical issues came first and she knew that as well as he did. 'Please. It's Dr Martin. I need confirmation about the medication.' He might have added that she should ask why the couple had been left alone like this, but he let that pass for the time being.

Following Beth's example, he touched Jean's arm lightly to get her attention. 'Beth is going to find out what's happening. In the meantime, can we make do with a pad and pencil?' Matt had noticed a ruled pad poking out of Beth's handbag.

Jean nodded and her lips formed 'Thank you', her hands signing at the same time. Beth grinned in response.

'You'll do. You have good lip patterns. Here you go.' She slapped the pad into his hand and disappeared out of the door, leaving Matt to share a laughing shrug with Jean.

Beth was gone for a while, and Matt spent the time questioning Jean about her husband's medical history and his current symptoms. Her answers, written on Beth's pad, were clear and concise, giving him the information he needed.

It wasn't that he had never seen a deaf patient before. But in the rarefied atmosphere of the fast track, he had never had to speak alone with someone who signed. And of recent years he had spent much of his time in the operating theatre, where it didn't much matter whether your patient could hear or not. Matt had come there to learn, though, and this kind of skill was as important as his well-proven clinical ones.

Beth still wasn't back when he got to the point where he wanted to examine Doug, but he managed well enough, even prompting a couple of encouraging smiles when he resorted to makeshift signs to indicate when he wanted Doug to breathe in and out. Finally Beth reappeared, the brief look that she shot at Matt intimating that she'd had some trouble finding Dr Martin. Matt drew the young doctor to one side and checked on the observations he had made, comparing them with his own.

He heard Beth laugh behind him. She was making a good job of seeming relaxed in front of Doug and Jean, but there was something forced in her tone that told him she was under stress. He dragged his attention back to the matter in hand and looked for a phone to arrange for a place on one of the general wards. He could have left it to someone else, but in his experience this kind of thing always happened slightly faster if someone senior made the call.

He returned to Doug's bedside and with Beth's help it took only a few minutes to recap on what he had already told them and explain that Doug's symptoms were severe enough to mean that he would be admitted to hospital. He would be in a general ward and a doctor would assess Doug's condition again in the morning.

Matt laid his hand on Beth's arm and she fell silent. She had been speaking as she signed, so that he could understand what she was saying.

He caught Jean's attention and spoke directly to her. This was a personal assurance and he wanted to make it himself. 'I will follow up on Doug in the morning and make sure that everything is explained to both of you properly. If you have any unanswered questions, I want you to contact me directly. We have to take every precaution, but Doug's condition is stable and you should try not to worry too much.' He pulled his card out of the inside pocket of his jacket and handed it to Jean.

Jean nodded to show she understood and her hand found his and squeezed it. A nurse appeared at the doorway, with a porter in tow, and he said his goodbyes to Jean and Doug and accompanied Beth out of the crowded booth.

'Are you or Marcie available tomorrow morning?'

'I'm not usually here on Fridays, but Marcie is. She'll be here whenever you need her.' Now that Doug and Jean were out of range, her tone was clipped and she was obviously angry about something. Matt wondered if she was angry with him.

'About eleven? Shall I call her in the morning?'

'No, that's okay, I'll speak to her. Thanks.' She had given him a half-smile, but it was clear that she was dismissing him, as if he wasn't wanted here any more. The tiny hairs on the back of Matt's neck started to prickle. No. She wasn't just going to send him away like this.

'How long are you going to be?'

She bristled visibly. 'I'll pop up to the ward in half an hour to make sure that Doug's settled in okay.'

Matt caught her elbow, exerting a fraction more pressure for a second longer than he needed, to indicate that he didn't want to hear any arguments. 'With me. Now.'

It wasn't fair. Beth knew that she had been

snappy with Matt when it wasn't really him she was angry with at all, but if anything that only made her more agitated. He put the two paper cups from the canteen down onto his desk, closing his office door and motioning to her to sit. Beth watched him doggedly as he stirred his coffee with the little wooden paddle that passed for a spoon. He was the one that wanted to talk about this, not her.

He took his time about it, but finally he broke the silence. 'I learned something tonight that I didn't expect.'

'What was that?' His conciliatory tone was antagonising her even more.

'I felt that I was the one at a disadvantage, not you or Doug or Jean.'

Warmth crept from her fingers, stealing slowly up her arms. She often felt that hearing people who could not sign were missing out in some way, but few would agree with her. 'Perhaps...' She left the thought unfinished. She *really* didn't want to talk about this.

'Look, Beth, I know there were mistakes made here. Doug and Jean should never have been left alone in that booth, not knowing what was going on. No patient should. But it happens. A and E staff work under pressure and with a constant set of conflicting claims on their time. They can't always stop to explain exactly what they're doing, they don't have that luxury.'

'So you're defending them!' Beth was shaking with an emotion that she couldn't quite define. She didn't want to hear Matt, of all people, telling her that it was okay to be confused and out of control of the situation just because you were deaf.

'No. I'm trying to find out what happened in there.'

'What happened is that the A and E doctor could have done more. You did. It didn't take much to explain what was happening to them.' Beth felt herself flush. He'd been great in there, caring and professional at the same time, and he deserved more than a grudging acknowledgement that sounded more like a criticism than a compliment.

The almost imperceptible twitch of his lips indicated that he didn't need marks out of ten for how he handled his patients. Not from her, anyway. 'I'm not saying that there isn't room for improvement.' He paused, running his finger speculatively around the rim of his cup. 'You're not just mad about this one incident. It's all the other times you've seen this happen that's got you mad.'

'Okay, then, yes, I'm angry.' She was sick of this. Every time the world reared up and smacked her in the face, there he was, ready to pick her back up again. She was tired of feeling his liquid blue eyes on her while she was struggling to cope with one sticky situation or another.

'So what are you going to do about it?' His question was quiet, measured.

'There isn't much I can do. As you just pointed out, it isn't necessarily anyone's fault. It's just the way things are.' If pretending that were true was going to end this conversation any sooner then she was willing to give it a try.

He laughed in her face. 'You don't believe that! No one with the kind of passion that you have truly believes they can't change things.'

'So what's wrong with a bit of passion?'

'Nothing. Do you think I don't feel it, too?' The sudden flare in his eyes, the way his lips curved slightly told her that he did. He might keep it firmly under control, but Matt Sutherland was no stranger to passion. She almost choked on the thought.

She could keep her mouth shut, but her hands betrayed her. *Okay, I feel it.*

He seemed to get the gist of her gestures. 'Then let me put my cards on the table. And perhaps you'll show me yours.'

'Let's see yours for starters.'

His fingers pinched the bridge of his nose in a brief expression of frustration and then he cleared a space on his desk, placing a thick document in the middle of it. 'This is the list of areas that I want to review in the cardiology department.'

'You'll be busy for a while, then.'

'That's the idea. There are a lot of items on here that are all about organisation and communication. If we can get that right, then I believe that it'll have real clinical benefits for our patients as well as improving their experience of our service.' He gestured towards a pile of files to one side of him. 'No-shows, for instance, which cause us a great deal of trouble and put the patient at risk.'

He stopped suddenly and flipped through the files. 'I thought Doug's name rang a bell. It so happens that he missed an appointment with me last Friday.'

Beth's heart thudded against her ribcage. This was awkward. 'I know.'

'You what?' He shot her a startled look.

'I know. Jean told me.'

'And you thought…what? That this wasn't a relevant piece of information that needed to be passed on?' Matt's eyes flashed dangerously.

'Jean asked me not to. As an interpreter I have a duty of confidentiality.'

'Not when the health of a patient could be compromised. The sole responsibility for clinical decisions is mine and I can't make them without all the information.' His control slipped slightly and he shot her a thunderous look.

He could rail at her all he liked, she wasn't going to back down. 'Yes, it is. But Jean was communicating directly with you and if she'd wanted to tell you there was nothing stopping her. She knew that you didn't understand signing and she had every reason to expect that her signed conversation with me was private.' Beth shook her head. There had been no obvious right answer to this and she'd had to make a judgement call. 'I know what you're thinking. If he'd turned up for his appointment then there's a chance that what happened tonight might have been avoided….'

He broke in, a note of exasperation in his voice. 'I don't *think* anything. I don't know what to think, because I've no idea why Doug didn't turn up for his appointment—for all I know he was being held hostage at gunpoint by the milkman. Don't *you* think it might have been sensible to mention it so that I could at least make some attempt to deal with the issue?'

'Yes, actually, I do. Which is exactly why I made Jean promise to discuss it with you tomorrow. She said I could tell you, but I wanted her to speak with you herself.'

He opened his mouth and then closed it again. The tension in the room snapped and the suspicion of a smile quirked his lips. 'Well, that's good to know, anyway. And for what it's worth, I think you made the right decision. I don't like the fact that they felt they couldn't trust me, but if the experience they had in A and E tonight is anything to go by, I can't blame them for not having too much confidence in us.' His eyebrows shot up as Beth's face betrayed her thoughts. 'What now?'

'Oh. Nothing. I was just thinking that you might have a point.'

He laughed. 'Well, I suppose we could go another round over that, but I'm willing to call it a draw.'

'Probably best.' Arguing with Matt had set her pulse racing, and the look on his face told her that the feeling was not entirely one-sided.

He scraped his hand over the back of his head. 'Look, I don't want to play games here. When you see Jean will you tell her that I remembered Doug had missed his appointment. That it's okay, I'm not going to label them time-wasters or put them to the back of the queue, but I would really like to talk to her about it because I want to know if there are things that I can do better.'

'Fair enough. Yes, that would be good. I'll tell her. Thanks, there are some doctors who wouldn't have taken that attitude.' It seemed that Jean and Doug needed no protection from Matt. 'So, anyway, was that what you wanted to talk about?'

He grinned, shaking his head. 'No. That was a side-issue.'

'So what's really on your mind?' Beth was feeling a bit more like listening to him now. She might even do a bit of talking of her own.

'I want to talk to you about the study you're doing. My deputy, Dr Allen, mentioned it to me and I found the proposal on the hospital intranet, along with some other papers that you'd written.'

He'd been checking up on her. A sensation that was not altogether unpleasant shimmered up her spine. 'Yes. I'm using computer modelling to isolate specific behaviours in doctor-patient interaction and relating them to the patient's perception of satisfaction and clinical outcomes.' She put an emphasis on her final words. 'With particular reference to the deaf.'

'I'd like to discuss the possibility of Cardiology participating in your study.'

What on earth was he up to? 'Why? Just because you have one deaf patient…'

'Actually, it's more than one, I got Phyllis to check. And it's not just about my deaf patients. I think that better communication can improve both our patients' confidence in us and our clinical outcomes. So it strikes me that I should be looking at whether the kind of techniques you're using will help us to assess our current communication strategies.'

He had to be under some misconception about what she was trying to do. 'It's only fair to tell you that your predecessor was resistant to the idea of me doing the study here in Cardiology.'

'Yes, I know what my predecessor thought. Phyl dug the relevant emails out of the archive for me. I don't agree with him. Both Sandra Allen and I think it's a great learning opportunity for the department.'

'But I don't know much about other groups. Deafness is my speciality.'

'Fine. All we want to do is to see how a study like this works. We'd like to be involved partners, rather than test subjects. But in return we'd give you an opportunity to try things out, see what works and what doesn't. We'd do what we could to get other departments interested as well.'

'How involved would you want to be?' Beth had a sneaking suspicion that Matt's idea of partnership meant that he would be in charge.

'That's up for discussion. But this is your study. You call the shots.'

Beth nodded. She'd have to see how that panned out in practice. 'I'll have to think about it.'

Matt settled back in his chair. 'Okay. What are your reservations?'

'Just one.' A great big all-encompassing one. 'I'm wondering why you chose *my* research.' Matt hadn't known her long and in that time he'd already seen her pathetically unable to cope and stupidly angry. Neither recommended her particularly as someone who would be able to run a serious, scientific study.

'I think that we could work well together.'

'That's a bit flimsy to base something this important on. There are a lot of other people interested in this field who are working with mixed groups that are much closer to your patient demographic.'

He grinned at her. 'Okay, then, if you want me to spell it out. I've read your previous papers and think that your research is excellent—meticulous and innovative. But what I want most of all is your passion.'

Beth wished he would stop talking about passion. Even the tips of her fingers were beginning to heat up. 'You called it getting mad earlier on.' Surely he couldn't be serious about all of this.

'Ah, yes, I did, didn't I.' His mouth twisted ruefully. 'I meant it, though. Problems don't just go away on their own, they need a bit of determined effort. I was rather counting on you getting mad at some point in the process.' It looked as if he relished the idea.

'Hmm. I might reserve my options on a little free and frank discussion.'

His eyes darkened suddenly. 'Be my guest. As much as you think you can handle.'

Beth's mobile chose that moment to vibrate in her pocket. She flipped it open, and there was a message from Jean. The last shreds of tension in the room dissolved, as more everyday concerns pushed their way to the fore. 'I've got to go now. But I'm very interested in your offer. Maybe we can get together soon to discuss it a bit more.'

He leaned back in his chair, hands behind his head as if to ease a knot of tension out of his shoulders. 'I'd like that. My diary's pretty much full, but it would be good to talk again before Christmas.' He hesitated. 'Perhaps I could take you out to dinner if you have a spare evening?'

No way! Dinner alone with Matt was a slippery slope that could lead to disaster. All the same, if she wanted to show him that she really was interested in his proposal, she had to come up with some alternative. 'Are you free on Sunday? I'm going over to Marcie's for lunch and you and Jack would be welcome to join us. She mentioned that she was going to invite you. We could talk then.'

'I'm not sure that's going to be possible. I haven't heard from Marcie.'

Beth bit her lip. He wouldn't have heard from Marcie. She had been supposed to pass on the invitation, but she had accidentally-on-purpose forgotten to do it. 'Well, she might have thought I was going to mention it to you.' She shifted in her seat, her cheeks getting hot again. 'I mean, I was, but I just hadn't got around to it yet.'

'In that case…' He still looked a little uncertain.

Beth turned his own tactics against him, and waved his objections away with a brief gesture of her hand. 'Great. You'll come, then. I'll let Marcie know to expect you both when I call her tonight, and she'll confirm with you tomorrow.' She rose and pulled the straps of her bag over her shoulder. 'There isn't anything you don't eat, is there?'

'No. Jack and I eat whatever's put in front of us. We don't turn down home cooking when it's offered.'

He'd let her off the hook and she grinned thankfully at him. 'I'll see you on Sunday, then.'

Before he could reply with anything other than a nod, she had turned to leave. Sunday would take care of itself. She had nearly two days to convince herself that this feeling of exhilaration was all about work and nothing to do with the infectious grin of the gorgeous Dr Sutherland.

CHAPTER SIX

THE roads were icy still, as the early cold snap continued. Christmas was approaching fast and lights and trees were beginning to appear in windows and along high streets. Beth arrived at Marcie and James's converted barn at one o'clock on Sunday, to find Matt's sleek, dark blue Mercedes already parked in the driveway.

Marcie ushered Beth through to an empty kitchen. 'Where is everybody?' The large open-plan space was uncharacteristically peaceful.

'Out back. James has taken Matt down to see the pond, and the kids have gone with them.' The old, silted-up pond was James's pet project at the moment. He and Marcie had bought and practically rebuilt the barn, turning it into a comfortable family home, and now James was turning his attention to the half-acre of land at the back of the property, which was currently a sea of iced-up mud.

Beth's eyes lighted on a large bunch of flowers, tastefully arranged and bound in raffia in a presentation box. 'Secret admirer?'

'Matt bought them for me.' Marcie brushed her fingers across the petals of a lily, which was the centrepiece of the yellow and white arrangement, and inhaled their scent, pulling at a piece of gypsophila that had become detached from its mooring. 'Nice, aren't they?'

'Lovely.'

Marcie was threading the stalk carefully back into the water and Beth left her to it, dumping her bags and the cardboard box she had brought with her onto the kitchen table. The box caught Marcie's attention and she flipped up the top and peered inside. 'Ah—one of your gizmos. For Jack?'

'Yes. I thought he might like it.' Beth pulled a large box-file from one of the canvas bags that lay on the table. 'I brought my research notes as well.'

Marcie puffed out her cheeks. 'Think that'll be enough? If you make him wade through that lot, he'll still be here to see in the New Year with us.'

'Well, I don't want him to think that this is not

already planned out. He's not going to just walk in and change everything to suit himself.'

'Hmm. Fair enough.' Marcie went over to the window and stared thoughtfully out of it. 'Do you think he's going to try?'

Beth shrugged, joining Marcie at the window. Matt and James were deep in conversation, James holding onto Anna's hand while the two boys played on the steep bank of mud that was to form the side of the pond. 'I don't know. He likes to get his own way.'

Marcie laughed quietly. 'And you don't, of course.'

Matt looked up, grinning as he saw the two women at the window, and Marcie gave a little wave. He always seemed taller, broader when not in a suit and tie, his shock of blond hair bright in the low sun against the dark leather of his jacket collar. James laughed at something he said, and Matt gestured towards the house. 'Looks like he's lost interest in the pond.' Marcie's quiet comment was accompanied by a wry smile.

'What do you think of him, Marcie?'

'It doesn't matter what I think.' Marcie had been uncharacteristically keeping her own council on the subject ever since last weekend.

'It does to me.'

Marcie sighed. 'I think he's a nice guy. Pete was always a bit too fond of being your knight in shining armour—making such a song and dance about how you needed him because you're deaf. I think he relied on it, to feel a bit better about himself. From what I've seen of him, Matt doesn't make concessions. He'll give you a bit of a nudge when needed, but he doesn't make a big thing out of it and he doesn't give you an inch the rest of the time.'

Beth raised her eyebrows. 'You've thought about this, haven't you?'

'Well, you did ask. Mind you, he does seem a bit distant at times.'

'You think so? I was wondering whether it was just me who thought that. But, then, he would, really, wouldn't he? With everything that's happened to him.'

'Yeah. Maybe.' Marcie was staring speculatively out of the window. 'We all have baggage, though.'

Beth ignored the observation. She didn't have baggage, she had hard-won experience. 'Well, sometimes baggage is just evidence of a journey.'

Marcie rolled her eyes. 'Sometimes.' She gestured out of the window. Matt had lifted Anna up onto his shoulders and was good humouredly trying to remove her hands from over his eyes. 'But look at him. Don't you think he deserves a chance?'

'Maybe he doesn't want one. He had the perfect woman. Mariska Sutherland's a pretty hard act to follow, you know. I don't think I'm quite in her league.'

'Oh, so there are leagues now, are there?' Marcie was grinning wickedly.

'Oh, stop it!' Beth laughed. 'Anyway, half the time we're arguing like cats and dogs. As soon as he starts telling me what to do, it brings out the worst in me.'

Marcie chuckled. 'Yeah, I imagine he likes a good fight. Anyway, I'm not suggesting you move in with him, just get to know him a bit. You never know, he might have some hideous hidden flaw.' Marcie stopped and regarded Matt for a moment. She obviously didn't believe it any more than Beth did.

'Yeah, like…' Beth looked towards the little group outside, which seemed to be about to come back into the house '…falling asleep halfway through a film and making you watch the second half again when he wakes up.' Marcie's hoot of amusement stilled Beth's hands.

'That's me you're talking about. James says he really hasn't seen a film unless he's seen the end twice.' Marcie turned from the window. 'Come on. Looks as if the hungry hordes are coming our way.' Matt was striding towards the house now, Anna perched on his shoulders, with James and the boys in tow.

There was laughter outside the back door and the thud of mud being kicked from Wellingtons, then James appeared. Three small blurs of activity followed him and finally Matt, standing motionless by the door. Beth managed a hello in his direction before she was surrounded by the younger members of the party. Anna and Josh received something each from her pocket and then Jack, who had been hanging back, got his parcel.

Matt was at his side in an instant, craning over the top of the little group of heads to see what was inside. Jack carefully took the tissue paper from the box and lifted out his gift, a blank look on his face.

'What is it?' The boy twisted his head around

to his father, obviously in need of some kind of prompt as to what he should do next.

'Here, let me show you.' Matt took off his jacket, pulled a chair up and sat down, pulling Jack into the circle of his body so that the boy could see what he was doing. Planting the gizmo in front of Jack on the table, he flashed Beth a wink across the top of the children's heads, seemingly oblivious to the havoc he played with her body chemistry whenever he did that.

He picked up the handle of the metal loop that was threaded onto a long, undulating length of thick wire. 'Look, you've got to move this loop all the way along here, without touching it against the wire.' Matt began to deftly move the loop along the twists and turns, his hand as steady as a rock.

'I bet your dad can't keep this up for long.' Beth grinned at Matt. He was altogether too good at this and Jack was not getting the idea. Matt jerked his hand, as if by mistake, and a line of coloured LED lights along the base pulsed on and off as the metal loop touched the snaking wire.

Jack jumped up and down, clapping his hands and babbling excitedly. He had turned to Matt and was tugging at his sweater.

'You give it a try.' Matt gave the loop to Jack, almost reluctantly, and watched intently as the boy took his turn. The lights flashed again and Jack wriggled with delight. 'No, mate, the idea is to stop the lights from lighting up. You have to get all the way along here to the end.'

Jack looked disappointed and Beth cut in. 'Something else happens when you get to the end.'

'What happens?' Jack's eyes were as round as saucers.

'Wait and find out.'

Matt was grinning as he ran the loop back to the start, ready for Jack to try again. 'It had better be good. He'll be playing with this day and night until he cracks it.' He tapped Jack on the shoulder as if reminding him of something.

'Thank you, Beth.' Jack responded to his father's prompt without even looking up.

'You're welcome.'

She looked up and found Matt's eyes on her, shining with approval. 'Did you make this? It's brilliant.' He gave Jack a nudge. 'Beth made this especially for you. No one else has anything exactly like this.'

Jack ignored him, concentrating on his new

toy, and Matt ruffled his hair, making the lights flash as Jack's hand wobbled. Jack moved the base of the toy along the table towards Josh so the two could play without any interference from the adults and Matt gave her an apologetic look. 'Seems he's too happy with it at the moment to say thank you properly.'

'Best thanks in the world.' Beth waved away Matt's apology with a grin and James wandered up, laughing quietly when he saw what Jack had.

'Beth's really clever with things like this.' He gave Josh a tap on the shoulder. 'Why don't you show Matt the puzzle box that Beth made for you, Josh?'

It was almost time for dinner and while Matt inspected Josh's puzzle box, Beth laid the table, moving Jack and his toy over to the comfortable seating area alongside the large oak table. She could see that Matt was genuinely puzzled about how to get the box open, and she grinned to herself. At last, here was something that he wasn't so clever with.

Lunch was the usual leisurely affair. Marcie had placed Matt opposite Beth, with Jack further down the table in between Josh and James. For once, Matt seemed to lose his nervous concern for his son, leaving him to enjoy himself at the other end of the table.

Matt had brought a very respectable bottle of red wine and everyone began to relax, faces and gestures becoming more expansive. It was nice to be here with friends—people who knew that in a crowded, noisy situation she might not catch everything that was said, and who didn't care if they had to repeat anything. There was no need to laugh at jokes that she couldn't catch the punch line to, or wonder whether she had said the wrong thing in response to a question.

Even before the meal had finished, Matt was talking about their project together, as if he couldn't wait to get started. 'It's so important that people with heart conditions understand what's going on and that I can reassure them. Stress and confusion can have a huge impact on how well they respond to treatment. I see the benefits of talking and listening to people every day and I'd like to do that better.'

Beth toyed with the apple pie and cream in her bowl. 'I just hope that I can help with that. It's a very tough issue.'

Matt flashed her a thoughtful look. 'It's tackling the tough issues that brings the most rewards.

It's just a matter of having the self-confidence to know that you're the right person for the job.' He returned to his apple pie, as if the comment was simply a general observation.

Marcie caught her eye across the table and Beth ignored her. If Matt had meant to make a point, it was forgotten now, his attention diverted to James, who was joking about Marcie's cooking.

'Main reason for marrying her. I was thinking of putting it into the vows, but I wasn't sure how that would go down with the in-laws.'

Marcie laughed. 'What, you wanted me to promise to love, honour, obey and cook the Sunday lunch?'

'Might have been more to the point. Actually, love, honour and cook the Sunday lunch. The obey bit was always a non-starter.' James winced as Marcie's foot obviously came into sharp contact with his knee under the table. 'Ow! See what I mean?'

'Well, I'm with James on this one. This pie is worth a marriage proposal all on its own.' Matt joined in the joke, nudging Marcie. 'Any chance of another piece?'

Marcie seemed immune to his charm and didn't so much as turn a hair under the warmth of his smile. Unfortunately she was also immune to Beth's look of silent entreaty. 'Of course, plenty there. Beth made half a dozen when she was staying with us last week and I put them in the freezer. I'll get one out for you to take home with you.' Beth supposed that Marcie could have said more but she didn't really need to. James nudged her knee with his under the table and her ears reddened with embarrassment.

Matt seemed completely unfazed. He made a laughing comment about cooks and broth that Beth didn't quite catch, which seemed to have had the desired effect because the tension around the table ratcheted back down a couple of notches and Marcie chuckled and dug him in the ribs companionably. Beth wondered what it would be like to be able to do that to Matt without wanting to follow up with a more intimate style of horseplay. Her cheeks started to flush and she dropped her gaze, fiddling with the hearing aid in her left ear as an excuse to cover at least part of her face with her hand.

Marcie took pity on her, and suggested that they take second helpings and coffee into the TV room, where they could talk more. Matt was bundled out of his seat and shooed through, despite his offers to stay and help with the washing-up, and Beth followed, her laptop tucked under one arm and her research notes cradled in the other.

She took her time getting settled, laying her laptop and notes out carefully on the coffee table in front of her, while Matt worked his way through the over-large second helping of pie that Marcie had cut for him. By the time she had poured the coffee, she was feeling a little more in control. Cool. Businesslike.

'Right.' She waited for him to finish the last mouthful of pie and put the empty bowl down in front of him. 'Let's get on with it.'

If Beth had thought that this was going to be a cosy, Sunday afternoon chat about some of the issues that she faced at work, she was mistaken. Before she knew it, the precious research notes had been handed over to him, and he was reading them through, closely questioning her on methods, control groups and almost every other aspect of her study. It was more thorough than the interrogation she had received from the grants committee, and he pinpointed all the holes in her reasoning, those she knew about and a couple that had not occurred to her.

Finally he slapped the pages shut. 'This is impressive.'

She looked up at him. He looked impressed as well. 'Thank you.'

'Can I take this away? I'd like to read it through again more closely.'

Beth hesitated. She wasn't sure that she wanted to give this to anyone at this stage, least of all someone whose opinion she cared about as much as Matt's. 'It's really still in development.'

'Understood. But this is enormously interesting as it stands.' He passed the document back to her, as if to emphasise that it was hers and she had complete control over it. 'Whenever you think it's appropriate, but I'd be really eager to have a copy.'

His praise was like standing under a cool waterfall on a sunny day. Little pinpricks of delight all over her body that made her shiver and grin like an idiot. Beth pushed the document back across the table towards him. 'This is a spare copy, I ran it off this morning. Just in case.'

He nodded, and took the wad of paper back, folding the pages of his pad carefully over it as if to protect it from harm. 'Thank you. Can we get together again next week to discuss what you might need from us to carry out your study in Cardiology?'

He was letting her in. And the grilling he'd given her had made it quite obvious that this wasn't just a favour to an acquaintance. Beth wanted to punch the air and dispense hugs all round, but currently the only person in hugging range was on her personal 'out of bounds' list. 'Yes, sure. I just hope that your confidence in me isn't misplaced.'

His long fingers caressed the pages of his note-pad. 'It's not.' His eye drifted to the pot of fresh coffee that Marcie had brought in for them while they'd talked and which had sat untouched on the table between them. 'More coffee?'

He filled her cup and the talk drifted. He seemed endlessly interested in almost everything about the study, wanting Beth to demonstrate the structure and syntax of BSL when she explained to him that it was quite different from that of English, and laughing when she showed him some visual puns.

'Well, I suppose that's one thing my deaf patients have in common with my hearing ones. They don't always appreciate my feeble attempts at humour either.' A thought struck him and his eyes darkened with mischief. 'So can you swear in BSL?'

'Why not? You can in any other language.' Beth signed a strongly worded invitation to reconsider his attitudes, which got a surprising amount of angst off her chest and had Matt's eyebrows shooting upwards.

'Right. Okay, probably no translation needed. I got the gist of that.' He flashed her a look of deep hurt, which melted into a smile. 'Did you just shout at me?'

He was getting the idea. 'Yes.'

'I think I probably deserved it.' He processed the information for a moment. 'So it's not just a matter of straight translation, is it? It's a different set of shared knowledge and ideas as well.'

'Yes, that's one of the things we mean when we talk about deaf culture.' Beth was enjoying herself now. He'd worked his way round to an idea that many people missed, doing it almost effortlessly. 'But you have to remember that most deaf people know the written language of their region and also the spoken one to varying degrees. Even if our first language is not English, it comes a very close second.'

'I realise I've never asked. What is your first language—English or BSL?'

'Both. My brothers and I grew up around signing and the spoken word together, so we all do both quite naturally. I never had that feeling that some people have that one is better or worse than the other—they're just different. BSL is a beautiful language in many ways.'

'So in your view one enriches the other.' He was nodding slowly, getting his head around the concept. 'Are both your brothers deaf?'

'No. Nathan is but Charlie is hearing. I have a CI and Nathan doesn't, but he does have more residual hearing than I do. So between us we're a pretty mixed bunch.'

'When did you get the CI?'

'I got by with hearing aids and signing help at school, but when the hearing in my right ear started to fail I really struggled at university. So I made the decision to have the CI and once I'd adapted to it, it was a revelation to me—a whole new world.'

'And the hearing you have in your left ear helps round the sound out?'

Beth nodded. 'Yes. I feel that I'm lucky. The CI worked well for me, which it doesn't for everyone, and I think I have the best of both worlds now.'

'That's a nice way of putting it.' He hesitated, as if he were choosing his words carefully. 'Something you said the other day surprised me. When you spoke about your deafness being inherited from your father.'

'Yes.'

'Does that bother you? You seemed... It seemed as if it did.'

'No. Why would it?' It didn't bother Beth in the slightest. It just seemed to bother everyone else and from his question Matt was no exception.

'No reason. I'm sorry if that was out of order.' He was staring at her now and couldn't have failed to notice that the temperature in the room had suddenly plummeted.

Beth reached for her laptop, snapping it shut, and started to gather the papers in front of her into a pile. 'Perhaps it's time we joined the others.' It had been a nice afternoon. She didn't want to spoil it by talking about this.

He hesitated and then rose slowly, picking up his pad. 'Yeah, okay.' He seemed about to ask something else, then thought better of it and let her lead the way out of the TV room.

When Beth entered the kitchen, it was all warmth and commotion. James was pulling on his jacket, and Josh and Anna were climbing on chairs to indicate the required height of the Christmas tree that their father was about to fetch.

Marcie looked up from the kitchen table, where she was showing Jack how to make gingerbread men. 'Hey, you two. All finished?'

'Just getting started.' Matt seemed suddenly pleased with himself and shot Beth a thousand-watt grin. 'What have you been up to, Jack?'

It was perfectly obvious what Jack had been up to. The apron he was wearing seemed to have almost as much flour and golden syrup on it as had gone into the dough, rolled out on the table.

'We're making gingerbread men, Dad. When we've baked them you can have one.'

'Oh, no, he can't.' Marcie stepped in briskly. 'No eating them until they're decorated.'

Jack quickly amended the offer. 'I'll decorate one for you, then, Dad.'

Matt's face lit up. 'Will you? I'd really like that.'

'You could do an icing stethoscope for its neck.' Beth winked at Jack.

'Oh, yes! And green icing for scrubs.' Marcie seemed more enthusiastic than even Jack was.

'I'm going to do one of Beth as well.' Jack was wielding the cookie cutter now and Marcie bent to guide his hand, and turn the dough figure out onto a baking tray.

Matt chuckled softly. 'Pink icing for her cheeks, then.' The comment was so quiet that Jack didn't seem to notice it, and Beth would have missed it if she hadn't been looking at him.

'Out! Out of my kitchen, you lot.' Marcie's voice rose commandingly above the hubbub. 'Anna, come and help Jack and me with these. And, Josh, perhaps you'd like to go with your father.'

Sensing that there was probably going to be something good to eat soon, Josh opted for the kitchen and James made a long-suffering face. 'Looks like I'm on my own, then.' He turned to Matt. 'Unless you fancy stretching your legs.'

'Yeah, why not? Where do you get your tree from?'

'There's a place a couple of miles down the road. Local garden centre.' James looked at his watch. 'They're open until six on a Sunday so we've plenty of time. Beth, do you want one as well?'

'Mmm, please. I'll bring my car. You won't get three into the SUV.'

James chuckled. 'I like to see a bit of pluck in a woman.' He turned to Matt. 'Last year we bought an extra one for the porch—just a little one. When Beth took off at a set of lights, it rolled out of the back of her car and I ran over it.'

Matt snorted with laughter. Beth braced herself for the comment and it never came. But of course Pete, who maintained that the only thing worse than a woman driver was a woman driver who couldn't hear when she crashed into something, wasn't around.

'What made you run it over, then?' He gave James a querying look. 'That's what brakes are for, mate.'

James threw back his head and laughed. 'I'll make a note of that for the next time I'm attacked by flying Christmas trees.' He picked up a jumble of elastic tie-down straps from the floor by the kitchen door. 'Think these will be enough?'

Matt nodded, grinning. 'Does this garden centre do lights as well?'

'Yep, and decorations. Do you need some?'

James handed Matt the tie-down straps and rummaged in the kitchen drawer for his car keys.

'Yeah, we don't have any.'

'What, none?' Marcie was looking at Matt as if he had just admitted to robbing a bank.

'Not one. My wife used to order a tree and it came complete with lights and decorations. After Christmas the company that supplied it came and took everything away.' Matt was studying the floor.

Beth wondered whether she should say something. She could hardly pretend she thought that a ready-decorated tree was a good idea, Marcie would never let her live it down. Luckily, the mention of Mariska seemed to herald a return to polite diplomacy on Marcie's part. 'Obviously a very well-organised lady. James, haven't we got some spare lights?'

'Yes, sweetheart, we have spare lights.' James turned to Matt. 'And if you'd take a set, then I'll be forever in your debt as I won't have to find somewhere to put them. What about that extra box of decorations that you never used last year, Marcie?'

'Oh, yeah, I'll get them out.' Marcie was in full flow now, and nothing was going to stop her, least of all any protest from Matt. 'It's just odds and ends, but if you get a few boxes of plain baubles, that'll be plenty.'

'If you're sure….' Matt turned to Jack. 'Something extra-special for the new house, eh, mate? We'll start as we mean to go on.'

Jack nodded vigorously and turned to Beth. 'Will you help my dad pick it out because he might not know which one to get and I'm busy here?' He indicated the gingerbread men that Marcie had been turning out onto the baking trays in front of him.

'Of course I will. We'll pick the one with the best top so that the fairy's nice and secure.' She stopped guiltily. 'Have you got a fairy?'

'You will have, as soon as we're finished with these.' Marcie winked at Beth. 'Will you people stop getting in the way here, when we've got things to do?'

It was seven o'clock before Jack climbed into his father's car, clutching the fairy that Beth had helped him make from an old-fashioned peg, some cardboard and a large helping of tinsel and glitter spray. Matt and James had taken it in turns to fuss over securing the two remaining

Christmas trees into Beth's car, and Marcie had produced a tin full of newly decorated gingerbread men.

Matt insisted that they drive to Beth's cottage first, and carried her tree around the side of the house, propping it up next to the back door. Then they drove together to his house, and Matt hauled the second tree out of her car, pulling the seats back up into position and, much to Jack's delight, slinging the tree over one shoulder before he carried it into the house.

'Come in.' It was not quite an order, but his tone was not without urgency. Beth looked at her watch.

'Don't you need to get Jack to bed soon?'

'Not for a while. And you don't suppose he'll go to bed before this lot's sorted, do you? Come in and have something to drink.' He indicated the tin in Jack's hands. 'I believe there's a gingerbread man with your name on it, too.'

'Okay. Just for ten minutes.' Beth didn't want the day to end yet. The look on Jack's face as he'd made his own Christmas decorations. The look on Matt's as he'd watched him.

Beth made the coffee, while Matt busied himself with the tree and the lights. By the time he had finished, Jack was already unpacking the box of decorations that Marcie had given them, sorting each one carefully according to size and colour.

'What do you think?' Matt stood back to assess his handiwork.

'That's fine.' Beth had abandoned her coffee, in favour of hanging onto Jack's arm to stop him from rushing over to the tree and starting to decorate it straight away.

'Maybe up a bit at that side? Do you think the tree's quite straight?'

'I think it's fine, and if you don't let Jack at it soon he's going to explode.' Beth directed Jack's attention to the ornaments that Matt had bought that afternoon. 'Why don't you put those on first, as they're all gold? Then it'll be easy to distribute all these different-coloured ones evenly.'

Jack nodded, choosing a small, sparkly globe and hanging it on one of the lower branches of the tree. Matt bent and retrieved the ornament, and hung it close to the top. 'You want the bigger ones at the bottom and the small ones near the top, don't you?'

Beth broke in. 'Actually, I think it looks better where it was.' She jumped to her feet, catching up two boxes of ornaments. 'Here, you take these…' she gave one box to Matt '…and Jack's in charge of these.' Matt wasn't going to end up with a perfect, beautifully dressed tree like this. He'd get something much better.

'Hmm. Yes, sorry, mate, Beth's absolutely right you know. Looks far better where you put it.' Matt retrieved the bauble from the top of the tree and put it back where Jack had hung it. 'Just let me know if you want me to lift you up to reach any of those top branches.'

Beth returned to the sofa and picked up her coffee mug. Just a few minutes to relax and then she'd be on her way.

Half an hour later, the tree was almost finished. Jack had enlisted Beth's help to hang some of his least favourite baubles around the back, where they wouldn't be seen, and Matt had taken over her place on the sofa, watching them.

'What do you say you and Beth put the fairy at the top together?' Matt carefully lifted up the fairy from her resting place on the coffee table and brought her over to Jack.

'Oh, no, you should do it. You have to make a wish.' Beth backed away from the tree.

'I'm all wished out.' Matt lifted Jack up effortlessly and sat him on his shoulders. 'Won't you help him? You must have something to wish for.'

Something immediately sprang to mind. Staying here, in the soft glow of the firelight, magic in the air and Matt at her side. Waiting while he put Jack to bed, looking forward to being alone with him, rather than just alone this Christmas. But her place was back home, in the quiet of her cottage. Not here.

'I've got something. I'm going to wish that…'

'No!' Beth and Matt both silenced Jack in unison. 'If you tell anyone what your wish is, it won't come true,' Beth explained.

'Okay, then. But it's something to do with…' Jack fell silent as Beth pointed a stern finger at him.

'You can't even hint. You have to keep it to yourself.'

'Are we ready, then? Jack, it's a fairy, not a model plane. If you wave it around like that, you'll get glitter all over Beth.' Matt rolled his eyes, holding out a hand to steady Beth as she climbed the stepladder to help Jack.

Carefully she guided Jack's hand and fixed the fairy to the top of the tree. 'There! Now, we'll all close our eyes and make a wish.'

Jack squeezed his eyes shut, wishing hard. Beth's eyes met Matt's and was caught in his liquid gaze. 'Close your eyes.' She whispered the words so quietly that she almost mouthed them at him. He had to have a wish. She wouldn't be able to bear it if he didn't.

He closed his eyes just in time. He didn't see her wipe the tear away as it dribbled from the side of her eye. And before he had a chance to open them again, she had hastened back down the ladder and turned away, so that she could no longer see what her heart desired most and which she knew she could never have.

CHAPTER SEVEN

BETH had only left the hearing therapy unit for five minutes, to run down to the canteen to fetch a drink. The receptionist was at lunch, Marcie was out doing home visits and Monday morning was always busy, so it was going to be lunch on the run again.

As she hurried back along the corridor, making a mental list of everything she had to do before three o' clock, she saw an unmistakable figure, leaning against the locked door of the unit.

'Waiting for me?'

'Nah. Just lost again.' Matt grinned at her. That confiding grin, the one that turned her insides to jelly and made her legs shake. The one that convinced her that everything else she had to do could wait for ten precious minutes.

'Well, you've come to the right person.' She motioned him away from the door and unlocked it. 'Come in and I'll point you in the right direction.'

He chuckled softly and followed her into the empty association area. Beth caught up a clean mug from the reception desk and tipped it towards him. 'Here. Want half my coffee?'

'If you can spare it.' He sat down, loosening his tie, slipping suddenly from mouth-wateringly formal to meltingly casual.

'I've only got time to drink half of it.' Beth tipped more than half of her drink into the mug and handed it to him.

'Thanks.' He took a deep draught. 'Just what I needed.'

'Busy morning?'

'Pretty much the same as yours, from the looks of it. I won't stay, I've just come to give you this.' He slid three typed pages across the table that lay between them. 'Just some notes I made last night, after I put Jack to bed.'

It was a great deal more than a few notes. Flipping through the pages, Beth saw an implementation timetable, noting dependencies and a critical path, and two closely typed sheets of suggestions and comments. 'Wow. That's great, Matt, thanks. You don't mess about, do you?'

His blue, thoughtful gaze was on her, trapping her in its depths. 'I have every confidence that this study is going to benefit my department. So the answer to your question is no. I don't intend to mess about.'

She could never get enough of this kind of praise from Matt. He could say it again if he liked, but Beth was aware that any hint to that effect would make her sound needy. She scanned the pages again, sipping her coffee.

'How's your week looking?' He'd given her a moment to recover herself and was moving ahead again. 'I'm leaving early for Jack's school Christmas concert tonight, but I can make any other evening. I brought your study up at the unit's weekly meeting this morning and there was a lot of interest. It would be good to meet up soon.'

He really did not mess about. 'Tomorrow would be fine. Here?' After last night, Beth didn't much want to meet with him at either his house or hers. She'd only just managed to get out of there before she'd made a fool of herself and shown her tears.

'If you like. Either here or in my office. About six?'

She laid her coffee down and grabbed at a couple of sparkly marker pens that she had knocked against and which were rolling towards the edge of the table. 'Yes, that would be great. Your office, perhaps. I imagine it's less of a mess than it is here.' She gestured towards the boxes of medical supplies and Christmas decorations that were waiting to be unpacked.

He grinned. 'Only because I haven't been in it for long. Give me time. Chinese?'

'I'm sorry?'

'We have to eat. I'll pop out and get a takeaway. I hear that the Chinese across the road isn't too bad.'

'It's very good.' Beth wondered whether a takeaway in Matt's office constituted going out for a meal with him, and decided it didn't. 'Yes, let's do that. Tomorrow at six.'

Beth made it down to his office at two minutes past six, and found Matt at the door, a large, fragrant-smelling bag with a red dragon on it in his hand. He grinned broadly at her and motioned her in.

He had cleared his desk, and set a comfortable chair for her on the opposite side of the desk from his own. He motioned Beth to sit, and put the bag down between them.

'I wasn't sure what you'd like so I got something of everything.' The side of his face twitched with tense amusement. 'I hope you're not picky.'

'No, I'm starving.' The food smelled great and Beth was hungry. She hadn't had a chance to stop for lunch and had made do with an energy bar from the bottom of her handbag.

'Good.' He seemed to brighten a little, and lifted his briefcase onto his desk, opening it and withdrawing two plates, wrapped in a dishcloth, followed by a couple of glasses.

'So that's what men carry in their briefcases, is it? I always wondered.'

Matt grinned. 'Yeah.' He tipped the open case so that she could see inside. There were files, pens, a stethoscope case, a toy car and something that looked like part of a model aircraft fuselage. 'Sometimes Jack's stuff gets mixed up with mine. The stethoscope's his.'

'And the car will be yours, then.' A picture of Matt and Jack sitting together in the evenings, Matt working on his files and Jack on his model aeroplanes, formed in Beth's head. She filed it carefully under 'Rose Tinted'.

'Yeah.' Matt spun the model sports car across the desk towards her. 'My first car was an old Spitfire. Leaked when it rained, needed a screwdriver and a lot of love to get started in the mornings, but it was my pride and joy.' He shrugged. 'Had to get rid of it, though. For some reason women seem to expect that driving somewhere means they won't get their feet wet.'

'Can't imagine why.' Beth leaned towards him. 'So you had an old Spitfire, you played in the rugby team and…what?'

He shrugged. 'Nothing, really. I worked hard, played hard. Thought that the world was full of possibilities. Just like any other young guy from the sticks who's just hit the bright lights of London.'

'Not so bright, though, when you get up close.' Beth could almost feel the claustrophobic, protective blanket of her childhood smothering her.

'Yeah. I gave the car away, to a friend who I knew would look after her properly, got myself a career and got married.' He made it sound like the end of all his dreams, not a bright new beginning.

'That doesn't sound so bad.'

'No.' He pursed his lips. 'Mariska smartened me up, stopped me from wearing grubby T-shirts and oil-stained jeans. Made me camera-friendly.' He shrugged. 'The paparazzi can be sharks, you know. When she died, they wouldn't leave us alone.'

'That must have been hard.'

'It was. I tried to protect Jack the best I could, but on the anniversary of her death they were waiting outside the house for us. We slipped out and I brought him up here, to my parents', for a week.' His face formed an expression of disgust. 'They wrote that we had gone away to grieve.'

'Instead of being driven away from your own home. Where you both needed to be at a time like that.'

'Yeah. It was then that I decided that we needed a new start. Somewhere where Jack could grow up, away from all the lies and pretence.' He stopped suddenly, shaking his head, as if he had said too much. 'I want him to be able to follow his own dreams and to know that it *is* possible to hang onto them.'

'What about yours?' This was so unlike the

Matt she'd got to know. The man who talked about passion with such fervour.

'Mine? Mine are for him now. With some left over for this place.' He shrugged and the dismissive gesture of his hand told Beth that his sudden candour was at an end. 'And at the moment I'm dreaming of food. I'm starving.'

He strode out of the office before she had a chance to reply, leaving Beth to start unpacking the bag of food. He was back in a couple of minutes, putting a bottle of wine onto the desk as he passed and then falling into his chair. There were tiny lines of fatigue at the corners of his eyes, which Beth hadn't noticed there before.

She picked up the bottle and read the sticker that had been plastered onto it, obscuring the label. 'Type AB positive?'

Matt's face creased in a weary grin. 'Yeah. Someone's idea of a joke. Fancy a glass?'

'Thanks.' Beth wiped the glasses with the tea towel and set them in front of him, while he fished a complicated-looking penknife out of his briefcase and extracted the cork from the bottle.

'We should drink to something.'

They should. To the evening stars, rising in the sky outside. Or to the velvet of his navy-blue eyes. To him locking the door and taking her in his arms, then sweeping everything that lay on the desk onto the floor and… 'Yes. Let's drink to the project.'

He nodded, and Beth thought she saw an echo of her own thoughts in his eyes. 'Good idea.' He tipped his glass towards hers, without touching it. 'To your research. And its successful implementation.'

They ate before turning their attention to work, Matt producing a couple of pairs of chopsticks from the bag. 'These okay? I've got a couple of forks somewhere.'

'That's fine. I'll manage.' Beth adeptly scooped a helping from one of the foil trays onto her plate.

He looked almost disappointed. 'And there was I with my rubber band at the ready.'

'You learned that way, too, did you?' The old trick of fastening the ends of the chopsticks together with a rubber band. The thought of Matt's fingers closing around hers, showing her how to hold them, was almost enough to make her lose interest in the food in front of her.

'Spurred on by a healthy appetite. Shame to see good food go to waste.' He delved around in one of the foil containers and produced a choice morsel, holding it out to her. 'Here.'

'Thank you.' Beth resisted the temptation to allow him to feed it to her, and took it with her chopsticks, depositing it firmly onto her plate. This was a working dinner.

After they had eaten, Beth went down to the canteen to pick up some coffee and when she returned Matt's desk looked once more like a place to work, the empty foil trays in the bin and those that they had not managed to finish stacked neatly on the filing cabinet. The strange light in his eyes remained, however, flickering as soft as candlelight as she opened her laptop and called up a new blank document.

'Shall I type?'

'If you don't mind.' Matt wrapped his hand around the cardboard coffee cup. 'I doubt if I'll be able to keep up with just two fingers.'

In the end, even Beth's fingers had trouble keeping up. His mind raced ahead, exploring possibilities and working through different courses of action. It was exacting, difficult work but she found herself enjoying it.

She ventured a few opinions and he listened carefully. A few more and he argued his case, giving in with a grin when she carried the point. Her confidence, usually shaky in these situations, began to grow and gradually self-assurance began to quiet her habitual craving for approval.

Finally, he looked at his watch. 'Nine o'clock. Suppose we'd better wrap this up soon.' He gathered the papers in front of him together with obvious satisfaction.

'Is that really the time? I'm sorry, I've kept you too long. You should have been home by now for Jack.'

He shook his head. 'Not tonight. My mother's looking after him and she'll stay over. And you haven't kept me, I've enjoyed this evening. You're pretty formidable once you get going, you know.'

Really? She'd never been accused of being formidable before but Matt had left her in no doubt that he meant it as a compliment. 'Well, thank you. I look forward to a return match.'

He chuckled. 'Me, too. I don't suppose you'd like to come over for a nightcap. We could talk some more.'

Beth shook her head. This was dangerous territory. Matt's house. Matt's mother. 'Let's finish off here. Go home and get some sleep. Tomorrow's another day.'

He looked as if he was about to argue and then he nodded. 'Okay. You're the boss.' Dark shadows of fatigue seemed to deepen in his face and he gathered together the papers that lay scattered across his desk. 'I'm hoping to get away on time tomorrow to spend some time with Jack, but if you have an hour or so on Thursday evening we could talk then.'

Beth nodded. That sounded a more sensible idea. 'Okay. In fact, there are some people I want to take you to meet. Say six o'clock?'

It was only a ten-minute drive to the university campus but Beth made it through the gates with a sense of relief. Her car was playing up again, and she had insisted she would pick Matt up outside the entrance to blue wing, not wanting to go through the rigmarole it took to start it with him around. Love might have worked with his old Spitfire, but her runaround needed a rather more determined touch.

She slid thankfully into the virtually empty car park and switched off her lights. The autumn term was winding to a close, and most people were out at parties or get-togethers before they went home for Christmas. Matt followed her over to the squat, ugly building that cowered in a slight dip alongside the main road, overshadowed by the tall, glass-clad Arts Tower and the elegant, turn-of-the-century Humanities block. Picking her way down a twisting metal set of steps that led to the lower ground floor, she banged on the only window that was illuminated.

Ed let her in, and Matt followed her through to the lab, a large dingy room, filled with desks and computer equipment. Beth hovered in the corner where the hum from the machinery disrupted her own hearing technology least, wondering what Matt would make of it all.

'This is Ed.' She gestured to the young man standing beside her. 'He's project managing and generally keeping me in order. And that's Luke and Allie. Luke's cracking out the code, and Allie's a linguist, so she's the expert on language definitions.'

Matt's eyebrows shot up. 'So you're…what, writing your own software?'

Beth grinned. 'Not entirely. But I couldn't find any existing software that would analyse my data the way I wanted, so we're making a few changes to existing modules.'

'Quite a few.' Allie was out of her chair, holding

her hand out to Matt and giving him an unusually bright smile. She was obviously dressed up to go somewhere, a short dress over leggings and boots, her long blonde hair falling down her back instead of tied up in its usual messy plait. Now that Beth looked, Ed was looking unusually smart, too, and only Luke was in his usual uniform of jeans and a washed-out sweatshirt.

'Hmm. Impressive. You have quite a set-up here.' Matt was looking around him with an assessing eye.

Luke's head snapped up from the screen he was studying. 'Yeah—wanna take a look at the new server?'

Beth doubted that Matt had the slightest interest in the server, however much processing capacity it possessed, but he was looking politely enthusiastic. Before she could step in with an excuse, Allie spoke up.

'We don't have time for that.' She turned to Matt, her hands clasped together in front of her, almost in a gesture of supplication. 'Dr Sutherland, we've put together a small presentation for you to show you what we've been doing to assist with the computer analysis of Beth's results. We know you don't have much time, so it won't take more than three quarters of an hour.'

So that was what Allie was all dressed up for. Beth had not meant them to go to all this trouble and Ed had said nothing about their plans when she had spoken with him the other day. She gave Matt a little shrug to indicate that she had no idea of what was coming next, and he gave her a melting smile, turning to Allie with an enthusiasm that belied the fact that he'd already had a long day.

Matt was silent as they walked back to her car later, as if deep in thought. As she drove out of the university entrance gates, gunning the engine to stop it from stalling, he woke from his reverie. 'What happens if they don't come up with the goods? To your research, I mean.'

'I'm not dependent on their software working. If it doesn't, there are other tried and tested packages that will do what I want, only not as well. Why, do you have doubts?'

'No. I think they'll deliver. They're a little rough around the edges, but there's no shortage of talent there. I was just concerned that you might not have a back-up plan.' He shifted in his seat.

'You didn't know they were going to make a presentation?'

'No. Sorry if it—'

'It was no problem. They saw an opportunity and grabbed it with both hands and I respect that.' He gave a small chuckle. 'It was a brave move to attempt a mock patient interview.'

'I thought so, too. We haven't done that before for real, only trial runs between ourselves. Allie was a bit enthusiastic about the symptoms.'

'If it had been for real, I'd have been calling for a crash cart.' His deep, rumbling laugh filled the car. 'I've never seen anyone that sick sitting up and grinning like a Cheshire cat.'

'Hey! It was just a demo…' Beth sprang to her team's defence.

'I know. And a very fine one at that. I noticed that you filled in a few gaps, gave them a bit of a steer when needed.'

'They had everything that mattered by themselves. I just added a bit of window dressing.' Beth wondered whether Matt was thinking twice about his offer to help with references and contacts when the three finished their doctorates.

'Of course they did. And I'm very impressed with them. They've worked hard and they're talented, they deserve to have their efforts shown off to the best advantage.'

'Yes. Thanks, Matt. You did them proud.'

'Did I? I'm pleased you think so. I can never quite get used to being someone that other people think they have to impress.'

'You mean you're still just a student at heart, struggling for a bit of recognition, just like they are?'

'Something like that.' He fell silent, watching the shadows cast by the bright mix of streetlights and fairy-lights as they slanted across the dashboard. 'Don't you miss it, Beth?'

'Miss what?'

'Being young again. Not necessarily in terms of years, but that feeling that the world's at your feet and it's all there for the taking.'

'They're twenty-two, Matt. I'm only seven years older than them and you're—what—fourteen years older? It's not exactly a lifetime.'

'Twelve, if you don't mind. But it seems longer, somehow...' He left the sentence unfinished and turned his attention to the line of cars in front of them, as Beth slowed to join the tailback.

'Dammit. I forgot that it was late-night shopping every day this week.' She revved the engine slightly. 'I hope my car doesn't die on me.'

'Having trouble with it?'

'It hasn't been the same since I got it back from the garage. Goodness only knows what they did to it, the engine keeps cutting out if I don't keep the revs up.' She turned to him. 'You might have to give us a push.'

'Oh! So you mean that you can't push and steer at the same time? I'm honoured that you think I'm that useful.' It may have sounded like a joke, but there was enough truth in the observation to make Beth shift uncomfortably in her seat.

'Don't get carried away. You're just a bit of spare muscle.' She revved the engine again, defiantly. There was no *just* about the well-honed frame sitting beside her.

'That puts me in my place, then.' His lips twitched provocatively. Matt Sutherland was definitely nowhere near in his place.

It was ten minutes of stop-start and then they were free of the traffic again. At least he'd refrained from giving any driving advice during that time, preferring to crane his neck at the brightly lit shopfronts and ask about the best places for Christmas shopping for Jack.

She put her foot down and reached the hospital car park without further incident. Matt had fallen silent, and seemed to rouse himself from his reverie as she edged into the parking space next to his car. 'So is there anything you would do differently? If you could go back and do it again.'

Beth got out of the car. There was one obvious answer to that one, but she didn't want to talk about falling in love and then being shoved unceremoniously back out again at the moment. It was about time she let go of that. 'No. I'm pretty happy with it all so far.'

'Really? You must have a clear conscience and a blameless life.'

He was standing too close and talking in riddles. Beth nudged at his shoulder in a gesture of friendly exasperation, and found that his arms were on either side of her, hands on top of the roof of her car, penning her in. 'Stop messing around, Matt.'

His eyes were dark, pools of shadow highlighting his strong features, yellow streaks from the overhead lighting across his face and in his hair. 'Is that what you think I'm doing?'

She wasn't sure what he was doing. She was

even less sure what she was doing. Beth reached up and her fingers found his jaw, running softly along it, feeling it flex at her touch. His lips moved closer to hers, still out of reach but they wouldn't be for very long.

Light blinded her. Someone's headlights, on full, sweeping around the car park. Matt moved to one side, using his body to shield her from the glare. After the car had roared past them, he leaned back on the bonnet of his own car.

'I'd… I think I'd better…' Go was the last thing she wanted to do. And exactly what she intended right now. Beth pulled her car keys out of her pocket and slid her fingers under the handle of the driver's door.

'So should I.' He didn't move, and Beth nodded. Climbing back into her car, she twisted the ignition key firmly and it started first time for a change. Must be a sign. She gave him a wave, and he returned the gesture as Beth backed out of her parking space and drove away. His figure leaned motionless against his own car as it receded in her rear-view mirror.

CHAPTER EIGHT

HE HAD nearly kissed her. Matt was not sure which he regretted most, that he had lost his resolve to keep his distance or that he had not finally tasted her lips against his. He held out as long as he could against the urge to talk to her and finally the rigours of the Saturday morning supermarket trip with Jack broke him. Pulling out his phone, he texted Beth.

How is your car? Can I pick you up this afternoon? M.

Matt thrust his phone back into his jeans pocket and turned his attention to Jack's current deliberations. He had announced that he wanted to buy Beth a box of chocolates for Christmas and was fingering a prettily packaged box of fairtrade, speciality chocolates that Matt had got down from one of the top shelves for him.

'These will be okay, Dad. I haven't got enough money, though.'

'Here.' Matt proffered a note and Jack whipped it out of his hand. 'We'll get her something nice, eh? Do you want to get her a bunch of flowers with the change?'

Jack wrinkled his nose. 'Flowers are for girls, Dad.' He rolled the note up and put it in his pocket. 'I'll just put these in the basket and see if there's anything else she'd like better.'

'Okay. Don't take all day about it, though, we've got some wrapping paper to get, too.' Matt lifted Jack up with one arm, so he could see the selection of boxes on the top shelf, reaching for his phone with the other hand as it vibrated against his hip.

Thank you, a lift would be great, car still playing up. See you both about 3? B.

It was guarded and she had made it obvious that this was all about accepting a lift rather than going to the party with him. Still, she had said yes. Matt found himself smirking with unconcealed triumph as he texted back his acknowledgement.

When Jack planted his finger on the doorbell, Beth opened the door almost immediately, as if she had been waiting behind it, although the comb and pins in her hand told Matt that she'd been standing at the large hall mirror, fixing her hair. His grip on Jack's shoulders tightened at the sight of her, as the earth tilted a couple of degrees on its axis.

'You look nice!' Her eyes were on Jack, and he felt the boy straighten in response to her appreciation. 'All ready for the party?'

Jack nodded. 'You look…' He was obviously lost for the right word, and Matt supplied it before he had time to think.

'Gorgeous.'

She coloured, dropping her gaze to the floor for a moment and stepped back from the door, allowing Jack to run into the hallway.

She was wearing a simple, mid-blue dress made of a heavy silk that followed her curves without clinging. Her hair was pinned up, curls escaping from a loose arrangement on top of her head that managed to look natural and sophisticated at the same time. Matt took in the blue pumps and the cluster of silver strands around her neck without really noticing them. As usual, her eyes drew his gaze. Wide, misty grey and like cool, inviting waters that he longed to plunge into. Surrounded by dark, heavy lashes that made them look even more ethereally beautiful.

Those eyes were registering apprehension at the moment. He summoned a friendly grin and stepped inside the house. 'Ready to go?' He tried to keep the tone light, but he couldn't help watching as she turned back to the mirror. The flexible sway of her waist. The pearly skin of her arms as she fussed with her hair, slipping the microprocessor on the side of her head under the dark strands so that it was barely visible.

Now he was inside he could smell her fragrance. Light, but not too flowery. Subtle, not the wall of scent intended to make you drop from ten paces that Mariska used to wear. Suddenly Mariska seemed out of place in his thoughts. Someone who was locked for ever in the past and not relevant to today.

'Nearly.' She stuck a diamanté pin into her hair, securing the last errant curl, and patted it carefully. 'That'll do.'

It would more than just do. Matt wondered what it would be like to carefully pull the pins from her hair, running his fingers through her curls as he kissed her lips. He'd bet his last pay cheque, along with all those in the foreseeable future, that her lips would be soft, and that her kiss would be tender.

She was saying something, but Matt had been too busy with the imagined kiss to listen. 'Sorry—what was that?'

'I said come through for a minute. There's a little something for Jack on the tree.' She held a finger and thumb up to give the measure of a token present.

'Oh. Thank you.' Matt turned to Jack and realised that they had left his parcel in the car. 'I think we have...' He was about to go and fetch Jack's present for him and then realised that he should let Jack do it. 'Here.' Matt handed his car keys to Jack without further explanation.

Jack trotted importantly back down the path, swinging the keys in his hand in what Matt realised was a pretty good imitation of his own habit. Beth was standing in the shadow of the hallway, watching him unobtrusively, and Matt looked through the open door into the sitting room.

'You've been busy! This looks a bit better than when I saw it last.' It looked great. Freshly cleaned and arranged, the room was inviting and homely, muted patterns, fabrics and furniture that didn't match but somehow managed to blend perfectly.

Her face lit up. 'Yes, almost back to normal now. When everything dried out the bubbles in the wallpaper in the sitting room and the bedroom went down, so I won't have to replace it. There's the hall to do over again and a new carpet for the sitting room, but I was going to get one anyway in the new year.'

'The bare boards don't look so bad. If you stripped and polished them, they'd look great.'

She pursed her lips. 'Do you think so? I've been thinking about that, but I'm a bit nervous about using a heavy-duty stripper.'

'Well, you need all the right protective gear but it's easy really. I can…' Matt reconsidered the offer. 'I was thinking of doing my study. Why don't you come over and give me a hand?'

She thought for a moment. Surely she wouldn't turn down such a well-concealed offer of help. 'Yes, okay. I can see how it's done, perhaps.' She giggled. 'At least I won't need any ear defenders.'

He wanted to hug her, but he was afraid that he might muss her delicate perfection. Or that she might slap him. Matt contented himself with walking over to where she stood, watching Jack as he pressed the remote to unlock the car doors.

'He insisted on choosing a present for you. And the paper as well. Wouldn't even let me in the room while he was wrapping it up.' Matt knew that she would value Jack's efforts far more than anything he could have done.

'That's lovely.' The tenderness in her face turned to mischief. 'I expect he didn't want you interfering with the grand plan.'

'Well, the grand plan apparently has to include reindeer, so I hope you like them.'

'As it happens, I like them very much.' Her eyes were dancing with mirth. 'Does that mean he's got to the end of the game I made?'

'More than once. "Rudolf the Red-Nosed Reindeer" is now well and truly burned into my consciousness. I found myself humming it during my afternoon clinic the other day.'

'Oops. Sorry.' She grimaced apologetically, clapping one hand over her mouth and laying the other on his arm. Even through his jacket, he could feel the tingle that seemed to race between them whenever they touched and the almost dizzy feeling that being in contact with her produced.

'Don't be. He loves that game. It's all the more special to him because you made it just for him.'

She nodded, obviously pleased. Jack was marching up the front path again, after having only half closed the passenger door of the car, but Matt decided to take the risk. Nothing was going to happen to it outside in the lane and now was not the time to interfere with Jack's efforts to be a grown-up.

The boy was unusually solemn as he faced Beth, holding out his parcel to her. 'Happy Christmas, Beth.'

'Ooh! Thank you, Jack.' She took the parcel and felt it carefully. 'I wonder what it is. I'm not sure if I can bring myself to open it, it looks so lovely.'

She caught his hand and led Jack into the sitting room. Matt followed, a few paces behind, stopping in the doorway. This was Jack's time with her. Maybe later on he'd get his turn.

Beth was perched on the comfortable-looking sofa, her present balanced on her knees. Waving her finger, she directed Jack to a little parcel that was hanging from one of the branches of the Christmas tree that stood in the window, almost completely obscuring it.

It was placed just low enough for him to reach, but not without a stretch. Jack dislodged a shower of pine needles and Beth only grinned at the mess. A sparkly gold bauble fell to the floor and rolled across the bare floorboards, making Matt wince, but Beth ignored it completely. Finally he managed to unhook the little red and green package and trotted importantly over to the sofa, plumping himself down beside Beth.

'Open yours first,' Jack insisted.

She professed further delight at how beautifully the present was wrapped, and opened it carefully, peeling the sticky tape off without tearing the wrapping paper. 'Oh, how lovely! How did you know that these were my absolute favourites?'

Jack's chest swelled with pride. 'Can I open mine now?'

'Yes, if you like. It's not as yummy as mine is.'

Jack tore at the paper on the package, and something fell out into his hand. He was busy deciphering a little piece of paper that had accompanied the something and Matt felt his heart twitch with suspense. What had she come up with this time?

Jack ran over to him. 'Look, Dad, it's a shark's tooth. It's a real fossil and it's millions of years old.'

'Wow!' Matt was genuinely impressed. 'Can I have a look at that?'

Jack pressed the tooth into his hand and capered back to Beth, flinging his arms around her neck, dislodging a curl of hair from its clip. Beth appeared not to notice, and returned his hug. 'Just think how big that old shark must have been to have had a tooth that size, eh?'

Jack thought for a moment. 'Probably about as big as a house.'

'I think so. Was it as big as your house, or mine?'

'Mine.' Jack turned to Matt. 'It was probably as big as our house, wasn't it, Dad?'

Matt nodded gravely. 'I expect so. We'll look it up on the internet tomorrow and see what it was like, shall we?'

'Yeah, Dad.' Jack took back his tooth and examined it carefully. 'Do you think it's a front tooth or a back tooth?'

Matt's gaze automatically flipped towards Beth, but she only shrugged slightly, her smile telling him that he was on his own with that one. 'I don't know, mate.' He hazarded a guess, based on nothing in particular. 'Perhaps it's a back tooth. We'll see if we can find some pictures on the internet.'

Jack seemed content with the rather lame answer, and Beth rose, putting her chocolates in pride of place on the mantelpiece. 'I'll put these up here where they're safe. Then I can enjoy them on Christmas Day.'

'So when you go away for Christmas, you'll take them with you?' Jack seemed concerned about the logistics of the operation.

'I'm staying right here for Christmas, so I won't need to.' Her eyes moved from Jack to Matt, and the brilliance of her smile hardly seemed to dim at all. 'Are we ready to go?'

'We're staying here, too, aren't we, Dad?' Jack had no compunction about making the observation and Matt wondered whether he might follow up with the question that was in his own mind.

'That's nice. I bet you'll have just as good a day as I will. And I'll be thinking of you when I open my chocolates, so it'll be just as if I was seeing you.' The firmness of her tone invited no further comment, and appeared to satisfy Jack, at least. 'Now, let's go, or we'll be late.'

Matt grabbed Jack before he raced past him and

did his best to tuck his shirt back in, hampered by a fair bit of squirming on his son's part. 'Hold on, mate, you can't go out with a lady like that.' Jack sighed and muttered under his breath.

Beth grabbed a dark woollen wrap from the hallstand and slung it over her shoulders, refixing her hair in front of the mirror. Then, collecting a small evening bag and a bottle-shaped wrap of tissue paper, she opened the front door. As he followed her down the front path to his car, Matt reflected that his son had beaten him to the punch and slipped his hand into Beth's.

Jack had insisted on carrying the box of cherry liqueurs they had purchased that morning, and presenting them to Marcie, while James received the bottles, peering inside the tissue paper and brightening when he saw the label on Matt's offering. Finally Matt had the opportunity to play the escort and pride rose in his chest as he took Beth's wrap, his senses quivering at her scent and the light brush of her hair against the back of his hand.

'Mmm. Nice decorations.' She looked around at the sparkly stars that hung from the ceiling in the hallway.

James grimaced. 'Yeah, I nearly broke my neck

getting them up there. Marcie insisted that they should go all the way up the stairwell.'

Beth patted his arm. 'Well, they look lovely.'

Matt had only wanted the one moment to play her date, and he'd had that, but he was greedy for more. He watched as Jack ran into the family room, where a little group of children were playing, and then resigned himself to letting Beth circulate, while he followed James to the kitchen to get a drink.

She turned and her eyes were round, pale pools of quicksilver, which put her jewellery to shame for lustre and hue. Before he could move she had slipped her hand into the crook of his elbow and wound her fingers around his arm. 'Come along, let me introduce you to everyone.'

Beth had no idea what she had been thinking. It was one thing to arrive with the newest member of the hospital staff, whose eligibility had already been assessed and discussed by the gossip machine. That could be construed as accepting a lift. It was quite another to take his arm and walk with him into the large open-plan sitting room. That would most definitely be construed as something more.

He'd looked so lost, though, standing alone in

the hallway after Jack had run off to play with the other children and what had started off as a friendly gesture seemed to have got out of hand. A dozen pairs of eyes were on them as soon as they walked in and she instinctively moved closer to him for protection.

Matt guided her over to where the food was laid out, and handed her a plate. His manners were impeccable, warm and attentive, but somehow indicating that this was the way any man would treat a woman and that there was nothing in it. She wasn't sure whether the sudden veneer was for her benefit or the rest of the room, but it gave the gossipmongers precious little fuel for further speculation.

She introduced him to the small cluster around the drinks table and he smiled and talked with everyone. Beth reckoned that it was about time she melted quietly into the background, but suddenly he snagged her arm.

The movement was so quick that it was almost imperceptible. His finger ran down the inside of her wrist and into her palm, staying there just long enough to make his meaning clear. He was not looking at her, but he moved slightly closer and she felt the soft cashmere of his sweater brush her skin. When he turned towards her, the look in his eyes was unequivocal. *Stay. You belong next to me.*

CHAPTER NINE

THE party was moving into its second phase. Easy chairs were pulled back to make way for dancing, and the bass notes of the music began to pump in Beth's head as James turned the volume of the CD player up. A child-friendly fruit punch was replaced with a killer concoction, which was Marcie's own invention, and she and James announced that the party was now for adults only by performing a practised tango across the sitting room.

Matt had left to drive Jack over to his grandparents' for the night and when he returned he was quickly lost in the crowd. It appeared that Beth no longer belonged at his side.

She shrugged to herself, biting back her disappointment. He probably wanted to dance or get to know people or whatever. Suddenly there seemed to be an empty space around her, even though the room was full of friends and acquaintances.

James caught her hand and pulled her into the group of dancers, while Marcie made for a young physiotherapist who was standing on his own in the corner. They were obviously both doing their usual job of getting everyone to join in, and Beth wondered whether she had looked as alone as she had felt.

'Having a good time?' The thud of the music was distracting her and James had to repeat the question.

Beth nodded, grinning.

'Matt having a good time?' This time James took his hand from her waist and signed.

Beth gestured over to where he was standing, deep in conversation with three of the nurses from A and E. 'Looks like it.'

James laughed. 'Bet he won't dance with any of them.' As if responding to a cue, one of the women tried to drag Matt into the crush of dancers, and he made an excuse, refusing to move. James flipped a querying finger in his direction.

Beth had caught the movement of his lips. 'He said he has two left feet.'

James's lip curled. 'We'll show him how it's done. Want to dip?'

Beth nodded, laughing, and James bent her

backwards over his arm until her spine cracked. He pulled her back up and twirled her round so that her head spun. When the room finally righted itself, Matt was nowhere to be seen.

James's finger tapped her shoulder, and she directed her attention back at him. 'Kitchen.'

She raised one eyebrow.

'Just in case you were wondering.' James's eyes were amused.

Beth punched at his shoulder and James laughed.

'By the way, you look very nice tonight.' He laughed, pulling her into him when she tried to stamp on his foot, and she relaxed against him, following his rhythm. This was nice. Warm and companionable. This wasn't Matt.

When James finally let her go, Matt was still nowhere in sight. Beth plastered a smile onto her face, helped herself to a half-glass of the killer punch and made the best of it. Just as well she had not had any expectations of tonight. She accepted every offer to dance, even the one from the hospital administrator who wheeled his partners around the floor like a perambulator. This was a party after all. She was having a good time.

Her head began to buzz, the white noise telling her that she needed a break from the sound around her, even though the party was not as loud as most. Making her excuses, she escaped to the kitchen to get a glass of water and some peace and quiet. Light was filtering through from the sitting room, and she didn't flip the switch for the overhead lights, preferring the cool semi-darkness as a welcome relief from the room she had just left.

A shadow detached itself from the far end of the room. Matt's lips moved but his voice sounded as if it was a million miles away.

'Hang on a minute.' She flipped the small control unit from its pocket, sewn inside her dress, and fiddled with it, setting the microprocessor back onto a setting that was suitable for the quieter environment. Matt waited until she had finished, watching her thoughtfully.

'Came out here for a break?' She could hear him better now, and she nodded.

'It's a bit loud for me in there.'

He set his glass down onto the countertop beside him and moved towards her. 'Want to dance?' He was still three feet away from her, but already she could feel a slow tingle, travelling inexorably up her spine. She shivered involuntarily.

'Not yet. I think I'll stay out here for a while.'

He nodded, never taking his eyes from her. He reminded her of a big cat, stalking its prey. 'I meant here.'

Beth looked around her. There was plenty of room and they were alone, but suppose someone found them out here. Dancing in a room full of other people was one thing. Dancing alone in the kitchen was something else entirely.

He seemed to sense her disquiet. 'It's okay. No one will see us here. I'll listen for anyone coming in.' His eyes flashed dangerously in the half-light. 'Don't you want to play hookey for a while?'

Before thought had a chance to intervene, she found herself mouthing 'Yes' and he took a step closer. She could almost feel him touching her, taking her into his arms. He made no move to close the gap between them, but waited for her, as if he knew she would come to him this time. His stillness, along with the mesmerising curve of his lips, only served to draw her in further.

As she touched his arm, she felt his hand slide around her waist, and finally he pressed her close to him. It was less a dance and more a kind of swaying embrace in time with the rhythm of the music outside. She laid her head against his chest, feeling his heartbeat, and her own picked up its pace, racing with it.

There was nothing but Matt, his clean, masculine smell and the feel of his body against hers. A long, low sigh escaped his chest, and she felt one arm tighten on her back, as if it might be possible to pull her even closer than she already was. The other hand began to caress her cheek, his fingers moving lightly across her skin, sending ripples of excitement down to her spine to meet the waves that were rolling up from where his other hand was planted.

His lips brushed against her temple, a soft sound of approval escaping his throat when she didn't flinch away from him. He knew that he had captured her, rendering her incapable of moving away from him, drunk with the heat of his touch.

When Beth tilted her head up towards him, his features were in shadow, but she could still see the look of almost agonised longing on his face. He circled her slowly towards the back door, his eyes never leaving hers, and somehow managed to get it open with one hand in the dark.

He caught up his jacket from the back of a chair, wrapping it round her shoulders, before guiding her across the threshold and out into the night.

Cold air hit her face, combining with the warmth of his body in a delicious interplay of sensation. Her back was against the wall of the house, his arms wound around her to protect her from any contact with the bricks. He kicked the kitchen door closed and they were swallowed up into the darkness.

'Beth, I…' He didn't seem to know what he wanted to say, just that he wanted to say something. She laid her finger across his lips, and they curved into a kiss. She raised herself up on her toes, pulling his head down to hers, and felt his lips against her cheek.

He dropped kisses onto her face, working his way slowly towards her lips. By the time he had reached them, she was almost breathless with anticipation. She felt a shudder run through him as he finally covered her mouth with his.

His lips became searching and then demanding, and when she didn't draw back, he deepened the kiss. He took his time, kissing her comprehensively, until her knees buckled and the only thing holding her up was his hand, planted on her back, holding her tight against him.

His hand moved a couple of inches downwards, from its place at the small of her back. Beth shuddered with excitement, wanting to feel his touch on every part of her body, thrilling to the thought of how his fingers might feel on her skin. One of her shoes had slipped unheeded to the ground, and she curled her leg around his.

'Beth.' Her name seemed to be enough this time. He kissed her again, taking the very breath from her lungs, taking everything that she had to give and then demanding more still. His body was hard, taut against hers and she followed the curve of his shoulders with her fingers, feeling the muscles flex at her touch. There was only Matt, only his demands on her, and the music of the party faded away, replaced by his name, echoing through the back of his head.

He broke away from her. 'Someone's calling me. The music's gone off.' He was still holding her, but it was more to support her now and he tilted his head, listening carefully. Then he bent and retrieved her shoe, putting it into her hand, and opened the kitchen door a crack.

He half lifted her through the door, closing it

behind them. 'Stay here. I'll go and see what's happening.' The kitchen was still in darkness, but Beth could hear voices outside. He strode quickly across the room, just as light flooded in from the sitting room and an urgent voice sounded.

'There you are. Come quickly.'

The voices receded and she was alone in the semi-darkness. Beth found a paper towel and scrubbed at her lips. What had she done? She'd got carried away, that's what she'd done. If Matt hadn't been called away...

She wasn't going to think about what might have happened. At least whatever it was that demanded his attention had saved her from doing something stupid, and given her a chance to resolve not to do it again. Ramming her foot back into her shoe and patting her hair quickly, she draped Matt's jacket back over the chair and made for the sitting room to find out what was going on.

Little groups of people stood around, talking quietly. Beth hurried through to the hallway and caught a glimpse of Matt, who was following James into the passage that led to the children's rooms.

No! Please, not the children. The tight movements of the two men told her that something was very badly wrong. Beth pushed past the knot of people congregated around the front door and followed them to the door of Josh's room.

Josh was lying on the bed, two of the A and E nurses at his side. They made way for Matt, who sat down next to Josh, one hand on his forehead and the other feeling for his pulse. Marcie was standing out of the way, in the corner of the room, her eyes on Josh, the material of her skirt twisted tight between her fingers.

Matt turned, and seeing her in the doorway shot her a tight smile. 'Beth. The keys to my car are in my jacket pocket. There's a medical bag in the boot—will you fetch it for me, please?' He didn't wait for her assent, but turned back to continue examining Josh.

She hurried to the kitchen and frisked his jacket, not pausing to feel inside the pockets, until she found the tell-tale bulge of a bunch of keys. Dragging them out from the inside pocket, she made for Matt's car.

It was as if everyone in Josh's room had frozen when she'd left and was in the same pose when she got back again. Matt sitting on Josh's bed, leaning over the boy. Kat and Nicki, the two A and E nurses, hovering close by, Kat on the phone and Nicki ready to react to Matt's instructions. James and Marcie were standing back, craning to see their son but not daring to get in the way.

Beth put the bag on the floor next to Matt and retreated back to where Marcie and James were standing. Marcie was near tears, and she slipped her hand into Beth's, her fingers squeezing tightly.

'What is it, Marcie?' Beth kept her voice low so that no one would be distracted by their conversation.

'I went in to check on him and he seemed very restless. I woke him up and he started to vomit—he's disorientated and complaining of a headache and abdominal pain. His pulse seemed very slow to me and we called Matt.' Marcie was whispering urgently, tears rolling down her face.

'Matt's here, Marcie. Josh couldn't be in better hands.' Beth wanted to tell her that he was going to be okay, but decided to concentrate on things that she knew for a fact. Such as if she hadn't been outside with Matt, he might have been here a few precious minutes earlier.

The silence in the room was crushing as Matt carefully examined the boy, turning him gently to expose his back. Finally, he pulled his stethoscope down around his neck, looking up from Josh. 'Any news on that ambulance?'

'Not yet. Half an hour, I think.' Kat spoke clearly, calmly. Beth knew that was a bad sign. She'd been in the company of A and E nurses and doctors on plenty of nights out before and they knew how to enjoy themselves. The only thing that would turn them this ice cool was if the situation was serious.

Matt turned to James. 'How long would it take us to drive from here?'

'This time of night—fifteen minutes, probably twenty.' Marcie broke in, her voice ragged.

'Okay, Kat, stay on the line and see if you can get any more information. James, Marcie, go and get your coats. We'll get ready to drive him in ourselves.'

Matt issued a few quiet instructions to Nicki, who set about wrapping the boy in a quilt. Kat held up her hand and snapped her phone shut. 'It'll be half an hour. Pile-up on the other side of town, they can't get to us any sooner.'

'Right. Let's move.' Matt straightened up and turned to face Beth.

Her hands were trembling. Whatever it was he

wanted to say would have to wait, there was no time now. 'Go, Matt. I'll stay here and look after Anna.'

'No, get someone else to do that. I think that Josh has ingested poison of some sort. Marcie says that he was playing with another boy this afternoon—Simon Tanner.'

'I know him. I think I saw his parents leave with him about half an hour ago.'

'We need to get hold of them. And I need you to look everywhere you can think of for anything that Josh might have taken.'

'But wouldn't it be better if Marcie did that?' Beth was ready to do whatever was needed but surely Marcie would have a better chance of finding something than she would?

'No. Josh needs her with him right now, and Marcie's too distressed to think clearly. I need someone who knows the house and the family and who can take a step back and think objectively.'

He was right. She was having difficulty in believing that Josh could be so stupid as to take something and Marcie would be even more dismissive of the idea. 'Okay. Do you know what I'm looking for?'

'Anything, but the kind of medication that might do this is digitalis or something similar. Check that this other boy couldn't have got hold of anything. It could be pills, or it could be plant matter—foxgloves are the usual culprit but that's unlikely at this time of the year.' He paused and looked back at Nicki, who was still tending Josh, and she nodded up at him. No change.

'I may be wrong and I hope that I am, but start now. Don't wait until we get to the hospital and get a confirmed diagnosis. Get everyone here to help, but make sure you check this room yourself. Tear it apart if you have to.'

Cool determination suddenly settled on Beth. She wasn't used to the pressures of emergency medicine, but she knew as well as any of the hospital staff how to cope with a crisis. Keep calm and do your job. 'Okay. Leave it with me.'

Matt nodded briefly, and looked round to find Kat at his elbow with his jacket. 'Great, thanks, Kat. Can you stay here? Beth will tell you what needs to be done.'

'No problem.' Kat waved him away, and Matt returned to Josh's bedside. 'What do you need, Beth?'

Right now she could have done with just one

more moment with Matt, enough time for a quick exchanged smile of encouragement. But that wasn't going to happen now. 'Can you co-ordinate? We need to get in touch with Simon Tanner's parents and make sure that someone's looking after Anna. Also someone to check on the other children, to make sure they're okay and see whether they know anything.'

'Okay, I'll sort it. I'll be in the kitchen if you need me.' Kat disappeared and when Beth looked back at Matt he was already lifting Josh carefully up in his arms, motioning to Nicki to follow him out into the hallway.

Marcie called to her from the doorway, her coat wrapped around her shoulders. 'Look after Anna.' Her face was anguished and streaked with tears.

'Of course. She'll be fine. Go.' Beth's encouraging smile dropped from her face as soon as Marcie was gone. Josh had looked in a bad way, half-delirious and retching, and Matt's reaction had told her that this was no run-of-the-mill stomach upset. Now it was up to her to find out what had made him so ill.

CHAPTER TEN

BETH hurried through to the kitchen, her eye lighting on one of the dispensary staff on the way. Grabbing his hand, she pulled him with her to where Kat was rummaging through the dresser by the phone.

'I've got Natalie organising a general look around in the main rooms of the house. Marcie's sister is seeing to the kids.' Kat had swung into action like a pro. 'I can't find Marcie's phone book, though.'

'In here.' Beth pulled the fat volume, held together with a rubber band, from one of the drawers. 'Simon's parents left about half an hour ago and they probably won't be home yet, but I expect there's a mobile number in there for his mother. Their name's Tanner.'

'Thanks. I'll be here if you need me. Good luck.'

'Think I'll need it.' Beth gestured towards the

medicine cabinet over the sink. 'The number for the combination lock is 7836—can you tell Brian what we're looking for? I'll be in Josh's room.'

'No probs. Go do your magic.' Kat winked at her, and Beth hurried back out of the kitchen.

Josh's bedroom smelled of vomit and fear. Beth flipped on the overhead lights and started with the bed, pulling off sheets and blankets, tipping the pillows out of their cases and turning the mattress to see if there was anything hidden beneath it. Turning her attention to the dresser and the wardrobe, she shook the piles of neatly ironed clothes out onto the floor, to make sure that nothing had been slipped in between them.

Think, Beth. The signs steadied her, old friends in a way that mere words never were, helping her to think clearly. *He knows he'll get into trouble playing with medicines. He's not going to hide anything where Marcie or James could find it.* That ruled out most of the house. *Every child has a hidey-hole somewhere.*

She picked up Josh's puzzle box, twisting it carefully until it sprang open. There was a ten-pound note, a stone with a hole through the centre, an assortment of what looked like broken pottery and some feathers.

Beth laid the box down on the small desk in the corner of the room and flipped through the contents of the drawers. The usual boy's mess of modelling clay, pens of every description and a hand-held games console, together with a few pages printed out from the internet that looked as if they were to do with Josh's schoolwork.

She ran her hands down the back of every piece of furniture in the room and dropped to her hands and knees to look under the bed. Nothing apart from a banana skin, a dusty harmonica and a toy train.

Beth puffed out an exasperated breath. There was nothing here. Josh usually took any mischief he was up to out of the house. *Coat pockets!*

She ran into the hallway, and elbowed her way through the coats in the cloakroom, finding Josh's parka and turning the pockets inside out. Nothing. A few sweet wrappers and some loose coins. She found herself wondering briefly how Josh had managed to make a hole in his pocket after only a few weeks of having the coat, and then an idea struck her.

Carefully, she pushed the pocket back into the coat, and slid her finger through the hole. It touched something inside the lining, and Beth wiggled it through the hole and pulled whatever it was out of the pocket. A penknife. It certainly wasn't Josh's. Beth knew that Marcie had been putting off buying him one until he was a bit older.

Beth inspected the lining of the coat thoroughly, to see if anything else was hidden in there. Then she stared at the knife in her hand. *He's up to something. And if this is hidden in his coat it must be outside the house.* Prising the knife open, she inspected the blade. It was dirty, discoloured, but there was nothing on it.

She picked up an old duffel coat of James's and Marcie's Wellington boots and walked through to the kitchen, where Kat was frowning into the phone. 'Anything?'

'Nope. Not home yet. I've tried the mother's mobile but it's going straight to voicemail.'

'What about the other children?'

Kat snapped her mobile shut. 'Anna told Marcie's sister that Josh has been playing with Simon, but that they wouldn't let her join in. Apparently they were digging for something at one point but Anna's pretty drowsy and isn't saying when.'

Beth dropped the Wellingtons onto the floor. Digging. What were those pages from the internet she had seen? She ran back to Josh's room and snatched them up from the desk. *Plan of a Roman Bath. Excavating a Roman Ruin.* James had said something about Josh having insisted that he had found some pieces of Roman pottery the other day.

She picked up the pieces of dirty clay from the puzzle box. Surely these couldn't have anything on them that would have hurt Josh? She sniffed at them tentatively, not really sure what she was trying to find, and put them back into the box. There had to be something more obvious than this.

Perhaps it was something else. Some kind of infection, maybe. But Matt didn't think so, and Beth trusted his judgement. If it was poison, it was up to her to find it, and her instinct told her that it wasn't inside the house.

Beth grabbed Matt's car keys from where she had left them on Josh's desk, and ran to his car, taking the lantern-style torch she had seen in there from the boot. Back in the kitchen, she pulled on the coat and boots and stuffed her phone, a pair of rubber gloves and some plastic bags into the pocket.

'Very stylish.' Kat was grinning at her. 'Going into the garden?'

'Yeah. Give me a shout if you hear anything.'

'Will do.'

Beth hurried past the spot where she and Matt had been together, just a few short minutes ago, taking the opportunity to curse herself again for her stupidity. Nothing good was going to come of it. Nothing good *had* come of it. He'd been out there kissing her when he should have been at Josh's bedside.

Her phone vibrated and the small screen told her that she had a text from Matt. Thank goodness. If he had the time to send a text then things couldn't be that bad.

Arrived hospital. Any news? M

She sent her answer quickly. *Ask James where Josh digging for roman pottery.*

Gripping her phone, Beth worked her way down to where the hole for the pond was being dug, wishing that she had thought to put find a pair of thick socks to put on. Marcie's feet were a size bigger than hers, and her stockinged feet were slipping backwards and forwards in the boots, making it difficult to walk on the uneven ground.

Her phone vibrated again. *Ten feet beyond pond. To the left. James was with Josh and Simon when they were digging.*

It was unlikely that they'd found anything dangerous, then. Beth swung the beam of the torch to the left and saw some areas of disturbance. There were some small pits, where Josh had been digging, and she carefully examined the area for anything that looked as if it might be the cause of Josh's illness. There was nothing.

She swung her torch around. There was some grass, a few scrubby bushes, but nothing that was either edible or poisonous. James would have rooted up anything that was that dangerous.

Beth almost cried out with frustration. What now? The garage lights were on and she could see men in there, looking around. It seemed that every part of the property had been covered and no one had found anything. Beth sank to her knees, feeling a trickle of water run into one boot. She had to think.

Of course she had to think, but not like an adult. She had to think the way that Josh did, look at things through the eyes of an eight-year-old. And she had to take a leaf from Matt's book, too, and not even consider the possibility of failure.

Okay, so what did she know? Josh had been digging at the end of the garden for what he thought was a Roman ruin. He'd been interested enough to go onto the internet and find out something about his subject. He had a penknife in his pocket and had collected pieces of pottery, stones, feathers...

Feathers! That could be nothing to do with a Roman ruin—Josh was old enough to know that. What did that mean? Suddenly light dawned. Jack had been talking to Josh last week about Robin Hood, and the two had been running around Marcie's kitchen, pretending to fire arrows at each other, until Marcie had called a halt to the game.

Beth swung the beam of her torch along the back fence and found what she was looking for. A hole, too small for an adult to squeeze through but big enough for a boy. Beyond the fence was open land and a shortcut through an area of woodland down to the main road.

She scrambled over to the fence. She could fit through the hole—just about. Beth dropped to her hands and knees and wriggled through, feeling her dress catch and tear on something.

Beth moved the torch beam around in a semicircle. Up against the fence, there was a collection of old planks and branches, which formed a small shelter. This was Josh's work. He had not just been engaged in digging for pottery, he had been doing some construction of his own. It was his own make-believe woodsman's shelter, an eight-year-old boy's version of something that Robin Hood might have built.

She walked carefully over to it and peered inside. There was a threadbare blanket, rolled up in the corner, wet from having lain on the ground. An old pot from Marcie's kitchen, a tin of baked beans and a metal tea caddy that Beth remembered Marcie throwing away some months ago. She could just imagine Josh here, playing in his own make-believe world. She reached in and picked up the tea caddy, opening it up.

It was empty. Tears of relief sprung to Beth's eyes and then she realised that she was no further towards finding anything. She swung the torch back and forth, looking for anything that might give some clue as to what had happened here.

'Stupid!' She signed to herself vehemently. Josh wouldn't be standing out here, he would be sitting inside the shelter that he had taken so much trouble to build.

Crawling on her hands and knees, gripping her phone as if it was a lifeline, Beth squeezed into the tiny space and sat down, planting the lantern torch in front of her. Reaching over to sort through the little cache of supplies, she felt something brush against her face, and when she leaned back, she saw two bare branches bent into the shape of bows, with pieces of garden twine for bowstrings.

The branches had been stripped bare, probably with the penknife she'd found, so it was difficult to see what type of bush they came from, but she took no chances. Pulling the rubber gloves from her pocket, she put them on and carefully unhooked one of the bows from where it was fixed to the ceiling of the shelter and examined it.

It could be yew, and it would be just like Josh to try and use the right type of wood if he was making a bow. And from what she remembered, practically every part of the yew bush was poisonous and could produce exactly the symptoms that Josh was suffering from.

She should let Matt know—perhaps they could do some test to either confirm her theory or rule it out. Crawling to the entrance of the shelter to get better reception on her phone, Beth caught sight of something. Hauling herself onto her feet and catching up the makeshift bow in her hand, she started towards a small clearing, surrounded by trees. She had not been able to see it when she was standing up, but at low level the red berries and dark green needles of a yew bush were easily visible.

She stumbled and fell as she ran across the uneven ground, but she was up again in a moment, hardly even feeling the pain in her knee. When she approached the bush, she bent low and saw that one of the branches was broken and hanging loose.

A quick inspection revealed several jagged cuts where branches had been hacked off at low level and when she compared the makeshift bow with the branches that had been cut, she found a match. It looked as if the branches had been cut recently, too, as the wood was still pale in the light from her torch.

Quickly she texted Matt. *Yew?*

She held her phone, staring at it, willing his response. It came immediately.

Possible. All symptoms in line with taxine poisoning. Do not touch.

Beth rolled her eyes. She knew that. The question was why that well-known fact hadn't occurred to Josh. Dialling Matt's number, she saw from the display on the phone that he had answered immediately.

She pressed the phone against her ear, straining to hear. Matt was saying something, but she couldn't make it out over the crash of branches above her head and the low howl of the wind. She spoke into the phone and heard him fall silent.

'I can't hear you properly. Listen and I will talk.' She repeated the sentence in case he had been speaking and not heard her the first time. 'I've found a shelter behind the back fence. Josh has been here and he's been cutting yew branches and stripping the leaves off to make bows. The cuts on the bush look recent. Text me back and let me know you've got this.'

Beth repeated her message again, but by the time she had finished, Matt had already hung up. Either he'd got it the first time, or he couldn't hear her at all. She stared at her phone and it obligingly vibrated in her hand.

Understood. Bring everything here. Use my car. Well done.

CHAPTER ELEVEN

BETH walked through the automatic doors into A and E to find Matt standing in the reception area, waiting for her. She handed him the carrier bag that she had brought with her, and he smiled.

'Good work. Wait here and I'll take these through.' He disappeared through the door to the clinical assessment unit and Beth was left alone again. She went over to one of the plastic chairs in the waiting room and sat down, inspecting her left knee, which was beginning to stiffen and throb.

Matt reappeared a few minutes later, walked over to where she was sitting, and squatted down on his heels in front of her, squinting at the graze on her knee. 'Let me see that.'

Beth had lost interest in her own aches and pains. 'In a minute. How's Josh?'

Matt shook his head but rose and sat down opposite her, drawing his chair up close so that his feet were planted on either side of hers. 'He's not out of the woods yet, but he's stable.'

That could mean any one of a hundred different things. 'What's happening, Matt?'

Matt leaned forward and took her hand. 'The doctors treating him have accessed Toxbase and are in touch with the National Poisons Information Service in Birmingham. They have enormous experience with this kind of thing, and they agree that it's probably taxine poisoning—which means that Josh has ingested some part of that yew bush. They have the option of transferring him over to the West Midlands Poisons Unit, but that's not necessary at the moment.' He squeezed her hand tight.

'Aren't they sure?' It all seemed a bit hit and miss.

'They have to act before the tests come back to confirm that Josh has taxine in his system. So we have to diagnose the old-fashioned way.' He made an attempt at a grin. 'Assess the symptoms and the probabilities and act accordingly. What you found out has helped a great deal, though, because we know what to test for and what the most probable cause of his symptoms is. They're doing a gastric lavage and Josh is on an IV drip to keep his fluid levels up, but the good news is that he's breathing on his own and his heart is steady at the moment.'

'And what's the prognosis?'

'The main worry is Josh's heart. He may experience periods of heart arrhythmia of various kinds, which, as you know, can be very serious. Or he may develop brachycardia—where his heart beats very slowly. If that's the case they'll need to consider transcutaneous cardiac pacing.'

'An external pacemaker?'

'Yeah.' Matt stared at the floor. 'The main aim of this is to keep him stable until the taxine is expelled from his system. He'll need to be kept a very close eye on over the next day or so, but there are very few deaths from this kind of poisoning, where people are not trying deliberately to do themselves harm.'

'And the other boy, Simon?'

'We don't know yet. I've just heard from Kat and she still can't contact them by phone so she's going to call the police to see whether they can send someone round to the house. In the meantime, we have to assume that the parents are awake and with the boy and that they'll get help if he falls ill.' A muscle twitched at the side of Matt's jaw.

'So all we can do is wait. Do Marcie and James know what's going on?'

'Yes, I explained it all to them and they're with Josh now. They'll probably transfer him up to the high-dependency unit initially to keep monitoring him, but I expect that he'll be taken down to the children's ward soon if everything goes well.' He paused. 'There's no reason to think that it won't.'

Beth nodded. 'Thanks. So…you got to him in time?'

Matt gave her a querying look. 'In poisoning cases, sooner is always better. But, yes, I hope so.'

She may as well say it. Now that she had nothing useful left to do, the nag at the back of her head had turned into a fully blown scream. 'What I meant was…would it have made any difference if you had been there a few minutes sooner? When Marcie first realised he was sick?'

Guilt bloomed in his eyes. The same thing had obviously occurred to Matt. 'Doctors can't live their lives constantly asking *What if.* It would drive you mad, you know that.'

'Yes. I just couldn't help thinking…' Beth could feel her face reddening, and was sure she was about to cry.

'Listen. If it hadn't been for you I wouldn't have even have been there. I probably would have taken Jack home and stayed there with him.'

'What?' Beth wasn't sure how to take this new information.

He sighed. 'I brought you to the party, remember. I wasn't going to just leave you there without a ride home.'

He was trying to make her feel better now. 'I would have got a lift from someone.' She'd done that very thing more than once, when Pete had wanted to go drinking with his mates after a party.

'Yeah, probably. But if I take someone somewhere, I expect to take them home again.' He shrugged. 'That's basic good manners, isn't it?'

'Yes, it is. Thanks. Let's not think about it any more.' Somehow they'd managed to get through this whole conversation without saying the one word that it all revolved around. Beth hadn't even signed it. The sign for *kiss* was far too obvious. She reckoned it was best to quit while they were ahead.

'Okay.' He nodded slowly. 'So now we've got that sorted, you need to get your knee looked at.'

'I'm all right. Really.'

'It's a nasty cut and it's absolutely filthy. And look there, you've got a slight swelling just below your patella.' He jabbed his finger in the direction of her kneecap.

Beth rubbed absently at the side of her hand, where she had been stung by a nettle. Her knee had started bleeding again and her stockings were ripped to shreds. 'I look a mess.'

Matt leaned towards her confidingly. 'You look beautiful.'

'No, I don't.' She knew full well that she was caked with mud, her hair was all over the place and her dress was torn. Beth tugged at the hem of it, pulling it across her legs.

His finger was hooked under her chin and he gently tilted her head up towards him. 'You do to me.' Large tears rolled down her cheeks and he produced a medical wipe from his pocket and wiped her face. 'Would you like me to take you home?'

Beth grabbed the makeshift handkerchief from him and blew her nose. 'I'm staying.'

Matt grinned. 'Now, there's a surprise. In that

case, we need to get you out of those clothes...'
He stopped suddenly, aware of the gaffe.

There was a moment of awkward silence and
then the tension broke and Beth began to giggle.
It was either laugh or cry at the moment, and
somehow laughing felt a bit more positive. Matt
shot her a conciliatory look. 'Okay. Bad choice
of words. Why don't you go and get a shower and
I'll see if I can rustle up a pair of scrubs for you
to change into?'

'You don't need to stay as well.' She wanted
him to. She didn't want to have to wait here alone
for news of Josh.

'Like I said, I take someone somewhere, I
expect to take them home again.'

'I can get a taxi.'

His lips twitched provocatively. 'I'll beg if I
have to.'

'You wouldn't know how.'

'I could take a shot at it. I'm sure I've seen it
done on TV.' He made a show of thinking hard.
'You get on your knees...'

'Don't you dare.' Laughter gave way to sudden
panic.

'Oh! Stop me from trying new things, would
you?' His face became solemn. 'Anyway, I said

I'd be sticking around for a few hours until Josh is stable. The doctors who are treating him have everything well under control, but they'll page me if they need me.'

'You might have said that in the first place.'

'I might.' He grinned. 'Truce?'

'Okay. Truce.' Just for tonight. While Josh's condition was still uncertain and Beth badly needed Matt's strength. Tomorrow she'd learn to stand on her own two feet again. And even if there were other doctors on call who could help Josh if his heart began to react to the taxine, with Matt here he would get the best.

It seemed that Beth, too, was getting the best. Although vastly overqualified for the job, Matt cleaned and dressed the grazes on her knees and smoothed antihistamine cream on the nettle rash, which ran halfway up her arm. Dressed in a set of scrubs that Matt had borrowed and a pair of sneakers from her locker, she began to feel almost normal, and the coffee and carrot cake that he fetched from the canteen finished off the job.

They waited mostly in silence, Matt sprawled next to her, his arm across the back of her chair. People came and went around them, a few of the staff stopped to smile and chat and slowly the time ticked by. One o' clock. Two. Beth felt herself being gently shaken awake, and opened her eyes to find James sitting opposite them.

He was smiling. That had to be good. Before she could ask the question, James had answered it.

'He's okay. Stable. They're transferring him up to the high-dependency unit now, and they're finding a bed for Marcie to stay over.'

'That's great, James.' Beth sat up, disentangling herself from Matt's arm, which had slipped at some point to wind itself around her shoulders and didn't seem to be responding all that well to her efforts to free herself.

James was rubbing his face with his hand, and Beth suspected that it wasn't just fatigue that he was trying to conceal. 'Thanks. Both of you. I don't know—'

Matt cut in with a dismissive gesture, and James grinned back. 'Yeah, right. You save my son's life and then sit in Casualty half the night and that's no problem.' He winked at Beth. 'This guy knows how to throw his weight around when he likes. I've never seen people move so fast as when he swept in here with Josh, issuing orders right, left and centre.'

Beth heard the smooth, rich rumble of Matt's laugh. 'It wasn't all down to me. There were a few other people involved, you know. Anyway, what matters is that Josh is getting the best of care.' Matt stretched and stood up. 'What are you going to do now?'

'I'm going to wait till Josh is settled and then fetch Marcie a change of clothes. I'll stay here as long as they let me then go back home so that I'm there when Anna wakes up in the morning.'

Matt shot a look of concern in his direction. The adrenaline that had been keeping James going had obviously subsided and left him exhausted. 'I'll drive you.' He held out his hand for James's car keys. 'I can pick up an overnight bag for Marcie and bring it back here.'

Matt was looking at Beth for confirmation. 'Matt's right. You need to go home and spend some time with Anna. We'll make sure Marcie and Josh are settled.'

James seemed unwilling to accede to the plan, but he could obviously see the sense of it and didn't appear to have the energy to argue much. Finally, after hugging Beth so tight that he nearly added a cracked rib to her other injuries, he disappeared for a moment to say goodbye to Marcie then followed Matt out of the reception area.

It wasn't long before Marcie appeared, alongside a bed with Josh's small figure curled up in it. Beth's hospital scrubs gained her entry to the HDU, and she saw that both Josh and Marcie were settled for the night, before she was shooed away by a pleasant but extremely firm nursing sister.

She supposed that she should go back down to A and E. She headed for the lift, and as she pressed the call button, the doors slid open.

'Matt! How did you get here?' He was standing inside the lift, an overnight bag in his hand.

'Marcie's sister dropped me back, and then went on home.'

'I meant how did you find the ward? It's a way away from your territory.'

'Ah. You mean it's not either the cardiology department or the canteen. I do visit other parts of the hospital from time to time, you know. One of my patients is in this ward.' He looked as fresh as a daisy. How did he do that?

'You've got Marcie's bag?'

'Yeah. I'll just pop it in now, won't be a minute.

I think it would be okay to take your finger off the lift button now, if you wanted.'

Beth jerked her hand away from the button, suddenly aware of the muted ding that repeated itself every couple of seconds. A blush rose to her cheeks and Matt laughed, slipping out of the lift as the doors closed.

'Stay there.' There was definitely a spring in his step that hadn't been there before. 'I need to talk to Josh's nurse for a minute, but I won't be long.' The last piece of information was hurled over his shoulder as he disappeared into the short corridor that led to the HDU.

He had seemed almost elated, but this was one occasion when Beth couldn't share his optimism. There was still another little boy out there who might be very ill and they couldn't find him. Now that the adrenaline in her system had peaked, dropped and then repeated the process a couple of times, she was heading fast towards an all-time low. She leaned back against the wall and slid downwards until she met the floor. Matt seemed to be taking his time.

He strode back around the corner and came to a halt in front of her. 'I've got some good news.' He reached down and grabbed her elbow, helping her to her feet, and for once Beth didn't have to think twice about leaning on him.

'What's that?'

'They've found Simon. The police were at Marcie's when I got there and they got a call to say that they've located him and he's okay. Kat took off with them, and they're bringing him into the hospital just to make sure. I don't know all the details but apparently he's confirmed that they did eat berries from that yew.'

'But he's all right? Wouldn't he have had some symptoms by now if he had eaten the berries with Josh?'

'Probably. There are a lot of variables in the equation and we have to be sure. But so far so good, eh?' He gripped Beth's elbows and she realised that she was shaking. 'We'll go downstairs and see whether they're there yet.'

He took her hand and called the lift, and she didn't pull away from him. She knew that she should, and that every small intimacy now would be paid for in regret later on, but it seemed that tonight's work wasn't over just yet. And until it was, the truce still held firm, allowing her to lean on Matt just a little.

CHAPTER TWELVE

THE reception of the A and E department was almost deserted, and Beth took a seat next to Matt, wondering whether they had missed Kat. A loud commotion at the door told her that they had not. Two policemen were flanking Kat, who was holding Simon's hand. His parents followed, arguing loudly. Matt took one look at them and was on his feet, making for the little group.

Simon was looking around cockily, completely ignoring his parents as they argued over his head, one of the policemen vainly trying to calm them. This was not good. The most important thing right now, for both Simon and Josh, was to get information out of the boy, and this was definitely not the way to go about it.

Matt slid in between the boy and his parents, effectively blocking his view of them and allowing Kat to guide him away. The A and E doctor who had been treating Josh hurried over and

Matt spoke quickly to him, then concentrated on Simon's mother, who was now crying loudly.

'Dr Sutherland says you know the boy.' The young A and E doctor was at her elbow now. 'Can you and Kat talk to him, while we try and calm the parents down?'

She'd try. From the look on Simon's face it appeared that his parents arguing like this was no particular novelty to him and he was obviously mentally removing himself from a situation he didn't want to be in. Underneath that cocky exterior he was probably scared stiff and would do his best to try and lie his way out of the situation if he could. Somehow, Beth had to get him to tell the truth.

Kat was walking Simon over to one of the consultation rooms, and Beth joined her. They took Simon inside and Beth closed the door behind them, while Kat sat Simon down on one of the plastic chairs.

Beth sat down opposite Simon, summoning up a cheerful smile for the boy. 'Hey, Simon, how are you doing?'

'Okay.' The one word was a start. She had to get Simon talking and then she could work her way around to asking him about the yew berries. Beth introduced Kat and as the two of them chatted cheerfully, she saw the pinched look on Simon's face begin to relax and he began to follow their conversation.

'You know, Josh and Simon have this great place in the woods—it's just like the one that Robin Hood and his men had.'

Kat looked suitably impressed. 'Wow. Wish I had something like that.'

'Me, too. I don't know what I'd do for food, though.' There was silence as Beth and Kat both pondered the question.

'You could shoot a deer and roast it on a fire,' Simon piped up.

'Ooh yes. Do you have bows and arrows, then? Proper ones, I mean. I heard that the best ones were made out of yew branches but I don't expect you can find those around much these days.'

'We made them. Proper ones out of the branches from a yew tree.' Simon was anxious to impress.

'That was pretty clever. How did you know it was a yew tree?'

Simon rolled his eyes. 'We looked it up on the internet. The yew tree has dark pointy leaves and red berries.'

'Well, that's very clever of you both. And I bet

that you and Josh had some adventures together, didn't you.'

'Yes, I saved Josh from being ambushed.'

'And did you find some things to eat in the forest?'

Simon nodded. 'Yes, we looked up all the berries and things that we could eat. Lots of them are poisonous, you know.'

'Are they? Which ones?'

'Lots. But the yew berries are all right, we read it on the internet. It wasn't them that made Josh ill.' Simon yawned, shifting in his seat. 'It said on the internet that the leaves and the seeds are poisonous, but the berries aren't, so we tried some.'

Beth shot a glance at Kat, whose smile had frozen on her face. Simon was quite right. Yew berries themselves were not poisonous. The seeds they had inside them were deadly, though.

'What did they taste like?' Simon didn't answer, and Beth tried again. 'I wouldn't have wanted to eat them, they probably tasted horrible.'

'That's what Josh said, so I didn't have any. So he dared me to eat something else.'

'I'll bet that was nasty. If I know Josh, he wouldn't have dared you to eat anything nice. What was it?'

Simon leaned forward. 'Peanut butter and mustard.'

Beth almost choked with relief and Kat came to the rescue. 'Ew. That's horrible. Did you eat any?'

'No. Josh's Mum wouldn't let us in the kitchen and then we had to go inside with the others and play a stupid game.'

Beth reckoned she had enough of the story to risk a few straight questions. 'So did you eat any berries at all, Simon?'

He shook his head. 'No, that was Josh's dare.'

'And how many berries did Josh eat for his dare?'

'Only two. I dared him to eat three but he wouldn't.'

Kat rose quietly from her seat and slipped out of the room, leaving Beth to continue talking to Simon, sleepy, inconsequential talk, just to comfort a small boy in a strange place. Before long, the A and E doctor returned with Simon's mother, who looked as if she had been crying. She flew to the boy's side and hugged him, choosing to ignore Beth completely.

Whatever. Beth didn't much care, she'd done

what she set out to do. She slipped out of the room, leaving them alone with the doctor.

Matt wasn't in the waiting room and she found him outside, leaning against the wall, staring up at the sky. The night was clear and cold, stars winking down at them. As the swing doors flapped shut behind her, he roused himself from his reverie.

'You were amazing tonight, Beth.'

His hand reached out for her, and she took a step back. Not now. Not any more. Now that the only thing left to do with the night was to go home, she'd be lost if she let him touch her. The delicate threads of their truce snapped.

'It was a team effort. Everyone played their part.'

He nodded. 'Yeah, they did. But you did something special. You made the link, found the source of the poison.'

'Thank goodness it's over, Matt. That everyone's all right.'

He nodded, his eyes glinting in the darkness. 'Yeah. It's over.'

That was the problem. Now that the emergency was over, the kiss hung in the air between them, refusing to be ignored. She'd told Matt that she wouldn't think about it any more, but now she couldn't help it.

'What happened, Matt. Tonight at the party. The, um…you know.'

'You mean when I kissed you.' He'd obviously been thinking about it, too.

'Yes.' Why couldn't she have just come out and said it, instead of beating around the bush like a teenager? 'It was just…well, these things happen at parties. They don't necessarily mean that there's…anything.'

'Yes. I'm sorry. Shall we put it down to the heat of the moment?'

'That's right. It was the heat of the moment. Thanks, Matt—for understanding.' She wrapped her arms around her body, trying not to think about the almost unbearable sense of loss that was pushing down on her. But this was how it had to be. She couldn't let her heart rule her head, not any more. She had to be strong.

'Come inside now, Beth, it's cold out here.' He pushed himself away from the wall, keeping his distance as they walked, as if he, too, knew the danger of a touch right now. He swung the doors into the building open and ushered her through, and the familiar, slightly antiseptic smell of the hospital hit her.

'Who did you get, then?' Perhaps if she talked about something else, her legs might regain a little of their strength.

'Eh?'

'Who did you get? Simon's mother or his father?' It was standard practice to separate people involved in arguments in A and E, so as to get them calmed down as quickly as possible.

'The mother.' Matt opened the doors to Casualty and scanned the waiting room. 'I think Kat's around somewhere, I'm sure she could do with a lift home.'

Beth nodded in assent, following Matt to the corridor that led to his office, while he flipped open his phone and briefly spoke to Kat. 'So what happened? Why did it take so long to find them?'

Matt rolled his eyes. 'Oh, apparently the parents had a row on the way home and she insisted he drop her and Simon at her mother's place. He went on home, but didn't answer the phone because he reckoned it was his wife calling and thought he'd let her stew for the night. Of course, Kat ringing repeatedly only made him more determined not to answer and so he pulled the jack out of the socket and went to bed to get some sleep.'

'No! So what about the mother?'

'Same thing. Only she'd already switched her mobile off so he couldn't call her. Anyway, Kat called the police, and they sent a car over to Marcie's and she went with them to the house, woke the father up and he told them where Simon was. And as you saw, the parents decided that this was a good time to start screaming at each other all over again. Kat said they were at it hammer and tongs in the police car.'

'Poor Simon. He's a good kid, but Marcie was saying he's been a bit naughty lately. Now I see why.'

'Yeah.' Matt pulled his office keys from his pocket and opened the door. 'The mother was in floods of tears, telling me it was all her husband's fault and that he was having an affair but he wouldn't admit it. Tomorrow she'll probably be telling all her friends what a terrible time she had when her son nearly poisoned himself.' Matt shook his head, catching his jacket up from the back of his chair. 'It tries my patience.'

'Well, I'm glad I got Simon. I probably would

have punched her. I don't know them all that well, but she and her husband always seemed so nice.'

Matt shrugged. 'Well, you never really know what goes on behind closed doors. Plenty of people are just playing at happy families.' There was a flat tone to his voice. 'Anyway, you got Simon to talk.'

'Yes. Kat told you?'

'Yeah. You know what worries me the most about it all?' Matt's face suddenly became drawn.

'That they looked the yew tree up on the internet, and read that it was okay to eat the berries?' Beth wrapped James's duffel coat around herself, before Matt had a chance to offer her his own jacket.

'Exactly. It's true enough, but it's misleading. And kids take things on face value. They don't necessarily think that the seeds are poisonous and they're inside the berries.'

Beth knew what he must be thinking. 'The statistics are in Jack's favour, you know. Despite all their efforts to the contrary, most healthy six-year-olds survive until they're old enough to know better.'

Matt's face broke into a broad grin. 'Yeah, I'm hoping to survive until I'm old enough to know better, too. All the same, I might just take a hammer to the internet box with the twinkly lights when I get home, though.'

'It's called a router, Matt. And he'll only go round to a friend's house and get onto the internet there.'

'I suppose so.' Matt scraped his hand across his head. 'Come on, let's get you and Kat home.'

They drove almost in silence, exchanging sleepy goodnights with Kat as they drew up outside her flat and then out of the city towards Beth's cottage. Her head was spinning. The party, Josh, Simon, Marcie and James. Matt. The kiss that they'd both decided meant nothing and they would forget about. What would have happened if they hadn't been interrupted?

The car drew up outside her cottage, and before Matt had time to switch off the ignition, she had gathered up the bag containing her things, was out of her seat belt and had the passenger door open. 'Well, thanks for the lift. I'll see you...' There was no arrangement to see him again. No reason to. Josh was out of danger, and Marcie and James were both tucked up and hopefully getting some sleep.

'Tomorrow. I'll call for you at twelve.' He

twisted his body across the passenger seat that she had recently vacated. 'If you'd like to pop in to the hospital with me, and see how Josh is doing.'

Beth hesitated. Of course she would like to visit Josh. The wisdom of doing so with Matt was questionable, but she was too tired to argue.

'It's a date, then.' Matt gave her no time to answer and she couldn't think of a suitable excuse anyway. 'Sleep well.'

He watched her walk up her front path, and flashed his headlights as she turned in the open doorway, waiting for her to switch on the light and close her front door before he drove away. Beth rested her forehead gently against the cool surface of the glazed front door, watching his taillights disappear up the lane, and then closed her eyes. So much for thinking that she had a bit more sense than Josh. Even he knew that if you played with fire, you were going to get burned.

Matt's car drew up outside her cottage at almost dead on twelve. Not irritatingly early, or fashionably late. It was as if he had been waiting around the corner for the hands of the clock to close at the top of the dial.

Beth had been waiting for him. She'd put her coat on, then taken it off again, thinking that it would look just a bit eager if she met him at the door with it on. Then, in the spirit of compromise, she'd put on a warm jacket, leaving the buttons open, to indicate that she might have just pulled it on when the doorbell rang.

In the end he didn't seem to notice what she was wearing. He was standing halfway down the front path, looking intently up at the front of the cottage, and he hardly acknowledged her as she pulled the front door closed and locked it.

'What's so interesting?'

'Up there, can you see?' She turned and felt him close the gap between them, his chest against her back as he stood behind her, his arm extended over her shoulder so she could follow its line of sight to a point just above the guttering. 'You have a couple of slates missing right there. I didn't notice it when I was up in your loft the other week, because the hole is located so low down, but it may be why the pipes froze. If there are tiles missing and the wind is in the wrong direction then it could well have been catching the pipes.'

Beth squinted upwards, shading her eyes

against the low sun. 'I see them. Thanks, I'll get them looked at.'

He turned abruptly and led the way to his car. 'Did you sleep last night?'

'Yes—and this morning. I woke up early, got up and then fell asleep again on the sofa while I ate my breakfast.'

'Me, too. Only my breakfast was a cup of coffee in bed, so I just rolled over and went back to sleep.'

That was too much information for a start. She could almost see Matt in his bed, hair tousled, eyes heavy with sleep. She wondered whether he slept naked or not and decided that it probably wasn't a good thing to think about that right at the moment, with him so close at hand. 'Well, let's go see how Josh is doing.'

Marcie seemed as bright as usual when Beth slipped through the curtains, half-drawn around Josh's bed in the bright, spacious ward, but there was a brittle quality to her smile. Josh was propped up in bed, his hand on the covers, still attached to a line that ran to the IV drips. His eyes were open, though, and he made an attempt at a smile when he saw Beth.

'Well, young man. How are you today?' Matt

was beside him, speaking softly and running a professional eye over him.

'Okay, thanks.' Josh didn't seem much disposed to talk, and his eyelids began to droop. Matt grazed his fingers across Josh's forehead, his eyes on the heart monitor by the bed, and gave a satisfied nod.

'He's much better.' Marcie took Beth's hand. 'Thank you both. For everything.' Since they had arrived in the ward last night, Marcie had developed the discomforting habit of not only thanking Beth in practically every other sentence but generally referring to Matt in the same breath as her.

'Wait until you see the mess I left at your house before you start thanking me. I turned Josh's room upside down.'

Marcie gave a tired smile. 'Didn't Matt tell you? James said on the phone this morning that when they got back to the house, the place had been cleared up and was like a new pin. Apparently, after you left, everyone set to and did it before they went home.'

'That's nice. Only what you deserve.'

'I don't deserve anything...' Marcie broke off and a tear rolled down her cheek.

Matt's attention was suddenly all on Marcie. 'Have you eaten this morning?'

Marcie shrugged. 'Not really. Few cups of coffee and a biscuit. I'm okay, I don't really want anything.'

He threw Beth a quick look and she nodded. Marcie needed to get away for a while. 'Look, Beth will stay with Josh for half an hour. Come down to the canteen with me. I haven't had anything and I'm starved. You can watch me eat if you don't want anything yourself.'

Marcie seemed unsure, but Matt was not taking no for an answer. He propelled her towards the end of the bed, and Beth slipped into the seat that she had been occupying beside Josh. Marcie gave in without too much of a fight, and let Matt lead her out of the ward, earning a swift nod of approval from the ever-watchful ward sister.

It was forty-five minutes before Marcie returned, and Beth had spent the time talking quietly with Josh and watching him sleep. She still looked tired, but she smiled as she plumped herself down by the bed, and Beth saw a flash of the Marcie that she knew.

'Okay?'

'Yeah. Matt made me eat one of the dreaded Danish pastries and told me a few home truths.'

'Oh. Nasty.'

'He doesn't pull his punches, does he? I thought that people were meant to be nice to the mother of a sick child.'

'And you would have listened to nice, of course. All this *I don't deserve anything, I'm such a bad person.*'

Marcie laughed. 'Well, when I found that stabbing him with the plastic cutlery wasn't going to work I gave in and listened to sense. Not that I don't still feel as guilty as hell, but wanting to exact horrible vengeance on myself isn't going to make things any better.'

'No, it's not. You love him, Marcie, and you and James have always done your best for Josh and Anna.'

Marcie poked the tip of her tongue out. 'Don't you start. I've already had that from Matt. You two haven't developed some kind of psychic link, have you?'

It felt a bit like that. The way they seemed to be able to communicate with just an exchanged glance. 'Well, if we had, I wouldn't need to ask where he's got to.' Beth couldn't see Matt in evidence anywhere around the ward. 'I hope you haven't left him slumped in a corner somewhere with critical head trauma.'

'No, he escaped that one. James turned up with Anna and they've gone to the Christmas grotto. Matt wanted to check it out and take Jack.' A thought seemed to strike Marcie and she switched her gaze from Josh for a moment. 'And by the way, where were you last night when we couldn't find you?'

Beth felt her cheeks flush. 'Sorry about that. We came as soon as we heard you calling.'

'Oh, not again. Matt's already been through all that as well, although he was shifty in the extreme when I asked where he actually was. What I want to know is whether I heard right when I thought someone said you were in the kitchen with the lights off.'

'We were outside.' Being outside in the dark seemed somehow more innocuous that being inside with the lights off. 'Matt was taking a look at the garden.'

'Right. The other one's got bells on it. So you went out there in the freezing cold to help him look at a half-acre of mud and grass. Sure that the lovely Dr Matt wasn't examining something a little closer to home?'

Beth shrugged. It was just a kiss. At a party. If she ignored it for long enough, surely it would simply give up and go away. 'Well, if he was it would have been the kind of mistake that I wouldn't admit to. Matt's a nice guy and a fantastic doctor. I don't want to ruin what could be a great friendship by getting into anything else with him. It's just too complicated, from his point of view as well as mine.' Maybe if she said it enough times, she'd believe it herself.

'If you say so.'

'Yes, I do. It's friends or nothing with Matt, I've made up my mind. I've got my life back on track now and I can't go through what I did with Pete again.'

Marcie sighed. 'Okay. But for what it's worth James agrees with me that the man's preoccupied with something…' She caught Beth's look of alarm and grinned. 'Don't worry, James isn't downstairs giving him the third degree. We confine our meddling to your life. Matt's out of bounds.'

It was another fifteen minutes before Matt appeared again at the entrance to the ward, his quick signal more than enough to tell Beth what was on his mind. There was a strict 'two visitors per bed' policy, and it was time to leave and let James and Marcie spend a little time together with Josh and Anna. Words, handshakes and hugs were exchanged, and Matt ushered Beth away from the couple.

'How is he?' Josh had looked better to Beth, but Matt was more qualified to tell than she was and she had noticed that James and Matt had stopped at the main desk to exchange a few words with one of the doctors there.

'They'll keep watching him carefully for a little while longer, do some more tests to make sure that the poison hasn't affected any of his major organs, but he's looking good. The first twenty-four hours is always the critical time in these cases.'

'I hear that you managed to get through to Marcie.'

'I hope so. Nice lady. I'll bet she has a hell of a right hook, though.'

'She didn't…' Beth had thought that the talk of stabbing Matt with the cutlery had just been Marcie's joke.

'No. She looked as if she was about to at one

point but we worked it out.' Matt flipped the fob of his car keys and the lights flashed. 'Do you mind a bit of a detour on the way home? Jack's with my parents today, and I said that I'd drop in and see whether he wanted to stay on for tonight. And I want to see whether my father has any roofing slates to match yours in his shed.'

Panic flared, making Beth's heart thump uncomfortably. Matt turning up at his parents' house with her in tow. On the other hand, they were just friends, so where was the harm in it? 'No, I don't mind. That'd be good, thanks.'

Matt's look of astonishment mirrored Beth's own surprise at her words. 'Right, then.' He opened the car door, waiting while she got in. 'Let's get going.'

CHAPTER THIRTEEN

MATT'S parents' home was a comfortable, spacious bungalow in a pretty village that lay only a few minutes' drive from Matt's house. The location was perfect, not so close that Matt was living in their pockets but not so far that Jack would not be able to walk or cycle it when he was a bit older. In their early sixties, the couple seemed youthful and active and were obviously extremely fond of their grandson.

She hung back a little, not catching the babble of conversation in the hall, and Matt turned to her. 'Beth, this is my mother.' He grabbed hold of her hand, pulling her forward, and Beth wriggled her fingers away from his grip. It was one thing to agree to come here on a whim, but now that she was actually facing Matt's mother nerves clawed at her stomach.

Jack was jumping up and down next to his grandmother, pulling at her sleeve, and she batted him away fondly. She looked at Beth, beaming.

'My grandson is teaching me how to suck eggs. He tells me that modern technology, which is of course quite beyond my understanding, allows you to hear me perfectly well. I'm instructed that I don't need to shout.' She poked Jack's shoulder playfully, her blue eyes dancing with mischief. 'That all right, then, Jack?'

Jack appeared to approve his grandmother's efforts and she held her hand out to Beth. 'Kate Sutherland. Pleased to meet you.' She grasped Beth's hand with a no-nonsense grip and didn't let go, leading her through to the sitting room, waving her into a chair and sitting herself down. The woman didn't just look like Matt, she had the same kindness and forthright humour and Beth found herself warming to her.

'Matt and his father are off to the shed.' Kate waved her hand towards the large picture windows at the back of the house, and Beth saw the two men, with Jack in tow, heading towards a large, brick-built workshop, situated at the end of the garden.

She peered at the structure. 'That's some shed. It's got bow windows!'

'Matt and his father built it the first summer that he was home from medical school. George salvaged all the materials and they spent a couple of months down there arguing about brickwork and roofing materials and goodness knows what else. Matt was at that age when they know everything.' Kate's eyes twinkled. 'I keep wondering when he's going to grow out of that.'

Beth grinned, afraid to either agree or disagree.

'They may be a while. Men and sheds, you know. So we've got time for a cup of tea.' Kate gestured towards a door that obviously led to the kitchen. 'Come and talk with me while I make it.'

Matt followed his father into the shed, noticing with some satisfaction that the pointing on the brickwork was still holding up against the weather.

'Nice-looking girl.' In Matt's opinion, his father always had been given to understatement. 'Got a good honest job as well.'

'Dad.' His father was taking a poke at Mariska now. Matt threw him a warning glance and looked over his shoulder to find that Jack had found something of interest at the far end of the garden and was well out of earshot.

His father shut the shed door behind him. 'It's all right, the boy's not going to hear. It might not be such a bad thing if he knew the truth about his mother, anyway.'

'Yeah. Right, Dad. I'll just tell him that when his mother died she was with her lover, shall I? I went along with the production company when they hushed it all up, perpetuated the lie because I didn't want him to know the truth about her. I still don't.'

His words had spilled out in a whispered rush. Even though the facts were unpalatable, it was good to be able to say even this much out loud.

'That's not what I mean.' His father was pottering around, picking up odd tiles and putting them back down again. 'He notices things, you know. Even if you think he doesn't.'

Panic flared in Matt's chest. 'Why? What's he said, Dad?'

'Nothing. But he will do. He showed me the toy that slip of a girl made for him and said it was better than anything his mother had bought for him. I thought it was, too, even if she did buy up half of Knightsbridge every Christmas. Had a play with it myself after he went to bed. Beat your mother at it fair and square.'

Matt grinned, despite himself. 'You're such a pair of big kids. Anyway, it's just a toy. Beth's good at that kind of thing, makes them for her friend's children, too. Mariska didn't have the time.' The comparison had been staring Matt in the face for a while now and he was acutely aware that Mariska didn't come out of it particularly well.

'Don't make excuses for her. She had the time for anything where there was a camera involved.' His father wet his thumb and cleaned a little patch in one corner of a slate tile, holding it up to the light so he could see its colour properly.

'What do you expect me to do, Dad? She was my wife.'

'She didn't act like it. And I'm not just talking about the affair you found out about when she died. Even when she was alive, you and Jack were never first on her list of priorities and the boy knows that. Beth shows more interest in him than his mother ever did. He talks about her all the time, you know.'

Cold fear clutched at Matt's chest. 'Look, Dad. Beth's been great with Jack and I'm really grateful to her. But I don't want him to start thinking that she's going to be like a mother to him, it's too much to ask of her. And he's lost enough already to be disappointed again.'

His father grimaced. 'There's nothing you can do to save him from being hurt. I learned that with you and your sister.' He glared at Matt. 'Particularly you.'

'Yeah. I never did quite realise how much you and Mum worried for us until I had a child of my own. I want everything for him, Dad.'

'I know. And for what it's worth I think you're doing a great job with the boy. But if you think that building your own world, where everything is the way you want it to be and you're in control is going to ensure his happiness, then you're wrong. You can only keep it up for so long before you start struggling with it and the boy sees that.'

Matt was stunned to silence. His father didn't often voice his opinions, but when he did he took no prisoners. He slumped down onto an old cast-iron safe that stood by the doorway and stared hard at some wood shavings on the floor.

He felt his father's hand on his shoulder. 'It's not your fault, you know.'

'It was my marriage. I let it fail. I didn't give her what she needed.'

'She needed attention. Not just from you, from everyone. You treated her like a queen and she still wanted more. Even her own son wasn't enough for her.'

Matt shook his head. There was more to it than that, but even his father didn't know the whole truth. Only he and Mariska. And she was dead now and that left just him.

Or did it? He'd reckoned that Jack had been too young. The thought that his son might be carrying even a portion of the burden that weighed him down, drowning him in deep waters, was too much to bear. 'How do I make it up to him, Dad?'

His father sat down next to him on the corner of the safe, and Matt slid to one side to make room for him. 'Let it go, lad. What's done is done. If you leave it where it ought to be, in the past, then you and the boy can both move on.'

Dad hadn't called him *lad* since he was a teenager. A lump rose in Matt's throat and he swallowed it back down again. 'I wish I could. I'm just not sure that I know how to change.'

His father barked out a laugh. 'Well, I'm not

the one to ask about that. Try your mother and let me know what she says. Now, go and fetch that girl of yours.'

'What do you want Beth for?' Dad was in an unusually loquacious mood this afternoon and goodness only knew what he might say to Beth. 'And she's not *my* girl.'

The denial came too late to be even slightly convincing, but his father let it go. 'Someone's going to have to tell me which of these slates will match what's already up there. Since it's her roof and she's a damn sight prettier than you are, I reckon you'd better go and fetch her.'

Matt opened the back door softly, to hear Beth describing how Josh had thought that yew berries were safe to eat. No doubt Mum had managed to extract full details of her job, where she lived, what she was doing for Christmas and whether she had any pets by now.

'Oh, that poor woman.' His mother looked up and saw him in the doorway. 'Hello, darling. Beth was just telling me about your adventures last night.' She turned back to Beth and leaned towards her. 'You know, when Matt was about that age he was fascinated by astronomy and decided that he was going to spend all night up on the garage roof, star-gazing. He got up out of bed and climbed up there and lay on his back, so no one could see him.'

'Mother…' Matt could feel the back of his neck reddening and Beth giggled. His mother warmed to her theme.

'Anyway, when we found that he was gone, of course all hell broke loose. We looked for him everywhere, calling for him, and when he heard us he tried to sneak back down on the other side, away from the house. He fell and broke his arm and we spent all night in Casualty, getting it X-rayed and plastered. It was then that he decided that star-gazing wasn't for him and he was going to be a doctor.'

Matt tried to look annoyed, but the sight of Beth, her face full of laughter, disarmed him completely. She was luminous—almost joyful— and obviously having a good time. Maybe now she wouldn't baulk at coming to his home when his mother was there, as she had done so inexplicably before.

'Well, if you've quite finished with my youthful indiscretions.'

His mother looked at him, her eyes softening. 'There's plenty more where that one came from,

dear. I seem to remember that the years that followed were particularly fruitful in that respect.'

He grinned at his mother. 'And I suppose the
age limit on parents embarrassing their children
means nothing to you.'

'Maybe I should fetch Jack. He might be interested in knowing about this age limit.' Beth's
eyes were mischievous and she caught his mother's eye, laughing with her.

'Oh. Ganging up on me now?' Matt couldn't
help a chuckle. Mariska had tried that one a few
times but Mum had never quite been able to
get on her wavelength, however hard she tried.
'Anyway, Dad has requested the pleasure of
Beth's company. He wants to show you some
roof tiles, so you can choose what you want.'

She flushed a little more and jumped to her
feet. 'Oh. Does he? Yes, thank you, I'd like to
help choose them.'

Matt steered Beth firmly out of the back door.
By the time they reached the shed, his father had
cleared away the cobwebs from around the tiles,
and held one up to the light for Beth to see.

'What do you think, pet? Will that match all
right?'

Beth nodded uncertainly. 'I think so.' She shot

a questioning look at Matt and he shrugged. He knew his father well enough to stay out of this particular debate. 'Yes, it does. Will it be the right size, do you think?'

'Where do you live?' His father was rubbing his chin ruminatively.

'Just on the edge of Easington. It's the row of five cottages on the little road that runs behind the post office. Mine's the one on the end.'

'I know them. Very nice little places, solidly built. Yes, these will be just right.' His father nodded his approval. 'Take it outside now and just prop it up against the wall. We'll see if we can sort out which of this lot are the best.' He gave the tile to Beth and she didn't move.

'I can carry more than one.'

His father chuckled and reached for another couple of tiles. Matt leaned against an old door, his arms crossed. If she kept this up, his parents were going to try and adopt her. Jack seemed to have noticed that there was something going on and bounced into the shed, receiving a tile from his grandfather and following Beth outside.

'Right.' His father straightened up and Matt noticed that there was a slight stiffness in the movement. He would have to enquire into that later. 'We'll take the rest, then.'

It took an inordinate amount of discussion to decide which tiles were best and Beth seemed determined to listen to everyone's opinion. A decision was made, though, and as Matt carried the tiles through to his car, he saw Beth helping his father stack the rejects back in the shed, gently chiding him when he tried to carry too many.

When they were finished, they all gathered in the kitchen, Jack tugging on Matt's sleeve to remind him that he had something to ask. 'Is it okay for Jack to stay tonight, Mum? Apparently he and Dad have something they want to finish.'

'Of course, dear, you know we love having him. Are you two staying for supper?'

'I think we need to get going.' Matt shot a querying look at Beth and she nodded. The intimacy of their silent interaction always sent warm shivers through his body. 'If that's okay with you and Dad.'

'Yes, of course.' His mother moved over to Beth and took her hands between hers. 'It was lovely to meet you. I hope that I'll see you again very soon.'

It took them another ten minutes to reach the

car, because Matt's father had to engage Beth in a conversation about plumbing and then Jack had to say goodbye again. Finally Matt managed to wrest her from the grip of his family, and they started the drive back towards her cottage.

'Your mum's lovely.' Beth was still suffused in the warmth of his parents' welcome, and the way they had accepted her presence without question. 'And your dad's such a sweetheart.'

'Hmm? Yeah, I'm very lucky to have them.'

'Jack obviously likes being with your parents. It must be difficult for you when he wants to stay there instead of coming home.' Matt had seemed a little preoccupied since they had left.

'Sometimes. But Mum and I talked about it, and we both think it's important that he's not just ferried from one place to another like a parcel, to fit in with my life. He and Dad have been working on a model plane together for weeks now and I can't drag him away from that just because it happens to fit in with my timetable. Jack knows how much I love him and that he always comes first.'

'And that you're there for the things that really matter. Jack was telling me about his school carol concert and how you and your mum and dad were clapping louder than any of the other parents.'

'Of course we were. He was better than any of the other kids.' Matt became suddenly tight-lipped. 'And there are no excuses to miss things like that.'

'No. And you only get one chance at it.' One chance was all that Beth would have asked. Just the one, to dress up in her best clothes and watch her own child on stage. She wouldn't have cared if it sang or signed the carols, she would have clapped until her hands were raw. 'It's great that your mum and dad are so involved.'

'It's a lot to ask of them at the moment, but when his usual childcare lady is better we'll review it. Mum's telling me that they want to fill in on a regular basis, and if that works for them it'd be great for Jack. I don't want them to take on too much, though.' He swung the car into Beth's lane and it bumped along the uneven road surface. 'We'll see.'

It was going to be dark in an hour, and even though Beth had been asleep for most of the morning it had already been a full day. Matt seemed to have accepted Jack's decision to stay with his grandparents for the evening, and turned his mind to lesser but more immediate matters, carefully lifting the roof slates out of the boot of his car and stacking them in the front porch.

'Never does any harm to have a few spares.' He regarded the half-dozen slates with satisfaction and Beth noted that they were certainly a good match for the ones that were up there already.

'No, it doesn't. Are you coming in for a cup of tea?' She didn't want to keep him from anything important, and she had already had enough tea this afternoon, but the prospect of having him leave now was like leaving a film halfway through the action. After all the emotion, she wanted to sit quietly with him, talking about nothing for a while, let things come to some kind of conclusion.

'Well, I was thinking of putting those tiles up for you. It wouldn't take long and that extendable ladder you have would reach up there. We could get it done before the light goes and then you wouldn't have to think about it any more.'

He was trying to persuade her. This was a far cry from his usual attitude of riding roughshod over what she thought and doing what he reckoned was best. Was this yet another side of Matt that she hadn't seen before?

'Well—I don't know.' Beth had been about to accept his offer but a little voice at the back of her head was wondering how far she could push this.

He made a gesture of helplessness that almost broke her resolve. 'It'd be a minor miracle if you could get someone in to do it tomorrow. And it would set your mind at rest to know that the place is secure.'

It would. The voice told her that she could take this a step further if she wanted to, though. 'I could help you with it.'

He hesitated and then a grin spread across his face. He had lost this particular battle and even though it was probably a new experience for him he didn't seem to mind that. 'That would be good.'

They carried the ladder through to the front of the house, and Matt extended it to its full length, leaning it against the wall. With his height, he could reach the gap in the roof easily. They secured the base of the ladder in the hard earth and Matt showed Beth how to lean against it to steady it while he climbed. The hammer and roof nails that he had borrowed from his father were placed within easy reach, along with a couple of the best slates, so that she could pass them up to him.

The job didn't take long and Beth spent most of the time with her eyes fixed on Matt for any signs that he might fall. He seemed quite at home up there, working always within the range of his reach, never looking in any danger of falling or dropping something on her head. And the view wasn't bad either.

He gave a final shove with the handle of the hammer to see whether he could dislodge the tiles and pronounced them well and truly fixed. As his eye began to rove across the rest of the roof, Beth called a halt to the proceedings.

'Come down now, you must be freezing. I'll make us both something to eat.' That sounded suspiciously like an order, and he blinked down at her, but started to make his descent.

'Sure?'

This was ridiculous. That was meant to be her line. 'Yes, come along. You need to eat.'

She stood back to allow him to climb down the final rungs of the ladder. His smile was almost mocking as he folded the sections of the ladder back together again and watched her gather up the remaining materials from the ground, putting them away neatly.

'I'll stack the rest of the tiles in the back garden for you. If that's okay.' He was definitely making fun of her now and Beth bumped against him, giving him a friendly shove.

'I think that will be just fine.'

CHAPTER FOURTEEN

SHE had pulled some home-made pasta sauce out of the freezer and thrown it into the microwave to defrost. Nothing fancy, but it was filling, nutritious and didn't take too long. The dining-room table was covered with her papers and books, all filed neatly in piles according to subject and importance, so she called through to Matt to ask whether trays in the sitting room would be all right with him. His answer floated through from the sitting room but he didn't appear in person and Beth wondered what he was doing in there.

When she carried the food through, it appeared that he had been uncharacteristically doing nothing. He was still sitting on the sofa, watching the lights on the Christmas tree in the gathering dusk. He hadn't even moved to switch the overhead light on. She jabbed at it with her elbow and he seemed to snap out of his reverie, jumping up and flipping the switch for her.

'Here, let me take that.' He relieved her of the loaded tray, so that she could go back to the kitchen to fetch her own food. 'Smells wonderful.' He waited for her to finish with the Parmesan cheese and sprinkled some on top of his piled dish. Opening one of the bottles of chilled lager that she had brought in, he filled her glass and then set about demolishing the pile of pasta in front of him.

They ate in companionable silence. He seemed as hungry as Beth was and polished off the large bowl of pasta before she had finished her smaller one, setting the tray to one side and picking up his glass. Stretching his legs out in front of him, he leaned back, a picture of relaxed contentment.

'Thanks, Beth—that was great.' His eyes were watching her intently and Beth wondered whether she had tomato sauce on her face.

'What?' She brushed her fingers across her lips speculatively.

'I was just thinking… Well, I wasn't thinking anything, really. That's just so nice sometimes.' His eyes flicked around the room and settled on the Christmas tree. 'I love a bit of sparkle at this time of year. Seems to make the dark evenings worth it.'

Beth abandoned her fork and laid her tray down on the floor in front of her. 'Doesn't it just? Makes you feel that everything's all right with the world, even though you know damn well it isn't.'

'There's enough that's right to make it worthwhile.' His irrepressible optimism again. 'Josh will be home for Christmas if he keeps up the improvement.'

'That'll be nice. One of the best presents that James and Marcie could ever have.'

Matt nodded. 'What about you? You're staying here this Christmas.'

Beth had hoped that the admission had escaped his attention. 'Yes. My parents are staying in America to spend Christmas with my brother and his wife.' She grinned. 'So she'll be getting a bit of an introduction to the Travers family Christmas games.'

'And you're not going as well?'

'No. I don't have much time off over Christmas and I'd prefer to take a few weeks off in the spring and go then.' Beth forced a smile. 'I'll miss our family Christmas, but this year's as good as any to make the break.' There had always been an unmarried aunt or two who came for

Christmas when she was a child, someone who had nowhere else to go, and she didn't want to turn into one of those.

'So what are you doing? I thought I heard you say you weren't going to Marcie's.'

'No, I'm not. They need to be on their own this year, just the four of them. I thought I'd go to the hospital on Christmas Day. There's something very special about spending the day with the kids there.'

'Why don't you—?'

'I'm really looking forward to it.' Beth cut him short. She wasn't going to risk having to say no to the offer of the one Christmas that she really wanted. 'So what are you doing? Are you going to your parents'?'

Matt shook his head. 'No, it's all down to me this year. I got a bit sick of playing the wandering addition that got taken in somewhere and Jack and I decided to have Christmas in the new house. I've got my parents, my sister and her family all coming over on Christmas Day.'

'That'll be great for Jack. A proper family Christmas.' Beth stopped herself. 'Sorry. I didn't mean that. It can't be. Not without his mother.'

'Well, it'll be different, anyway.' Matt's mouth

twitched downwards for a second. 'Mariska used to like to go out for lunch somewhere smart on Christmas Day, and so Jack's used to spending the day on his best behaviour.'

That sounded a bit dull. Beth couldn't think of a suitable reply.

'Anyway, this year's going to be about what we want. I'm going to try my hand at a full Christmas dinner and just hope it's not too much of a disaster.' His tone was almost defiant.

'They'll love it. Anyway, I can't imagine your mum would let you burn the turkey.'

Matt grinned. 'No. Or my sister. I was thinking of barricading the kitchen door, but my sister will just climb in through the window and start stirring something.' He grinned. 'When she and Mum get together they're quite a force to be reckoned with. Both think they know what's best.'

'Which would make you the odd man out in your family?'

He chuckled, laughter lines replacing the stress that had appeared in his face. That smile was like a strong drug, and Beth was way past the point of just saying no. 'Actually, I am. I'm the one who listens to reason and always does as he's told.'

'Right.' Beth focused her eyes on the window

to make her point. 'Those pigs flying around up there are looking very festive with tinsel around their trotters.'

Matt laughed out loud, throwing his arm across the back of the sofa in her direction. 'Okay, you win.' He didn't move his hand, but his finger strayed just enough to brush her arm. 'If I disagree then you've just proved your point anyway. So I'll just have to be man enough to know when I'm beaten.'

This was past endurance. If the strong, capable Matt wasn't tantalising enough, his surrender was beyond any imagining. She saw a glimpse of those delights deep in his blue eyes, and almost choked on a rush of sudden need for him. Beth pulled away, knowing that she could no longer breathe with him this close, and picked up the tray from the floor, stacking the plates on it to carry them through to the kitchen.

Matt followed her. Without asking, he picked up a tea towel and waited for her to fill the sink. 'So tell me. Which of the Travers family Christmas games are your favourites? I can do with a bit of a steer for what to do after lunch on Christmas Day.'

'All of them.' Beth turned the taps off, swirling

her hand around in the hot water to froth up the detergent. 'Dad loves charades and he always cheats by signing behind Mum's parents' backs.'

'Making use of an unfair advantage, eh? They never learned signing?'

'A bit, when I was little. They're not very good at it.' She handed him a plate. 'I like Monopoly. Adult Monopoly is great.'

The soapy plate slipped a couple of inches between his fingers before he managed to regain his grip on it. 'Adult Monopoly?' It was perfectly clear what he was thinking. His heavy-lidded eyes were practically undressing her right there, by the kitchen sink. Slowly.

Beth was sure that she was blushing, but that didn't seem to deter him. At this point in time it wasn't deterring her much either. 'Adult Monopoly is where you don't have to be nice and let the children win. You can be as much of a double-dealing shark of a property developer as you like.'

Light dawned and he nodded. 'You want to show me how that's done?'

Beth showed him how it was done all right. After they had stacked the plates away, she laid out her old, battered Monopoly board between them on the coffee table, and counted out the money. Whitechapel and Old Kent Road fell to Matt, and he began to build up a small empire of houses and hotels, but Beth managed to secure Mayfair from right under his nose. Matt spent an inordinately long time cooling his heels in jail, and then staged a late comeback, capturing both Leicester Square and Piccadilly in one circuit.

'There! That'll be four hundred and fifty pounds, please.' He surveyed her diminished stack of money with satisfaction.

'Of course.' Beth reached behind her and drew out the money that she had been building up under the sofa cushions.

'No! That's cheating!'

'No, it's not. I just put a little away for a rainy day. Call it an offshore account for tax purposes.' She counted the money out onto the board and pushed the dice towards him. Fleet Street and its houses and hotel lay between his counter and Go.

Matt shook the dice and she squealed with delight. 'Aha! Gotcha! That'll be…' She calculated quickly in her head. 'One thousand five hundred pounds. And no IOUs'

He counted out his stack of money. 'I'm only a

hundred pounds short. You're not going to fore-
close on me for that, are you?'

'You bet your sweet life I am. Come on, pay
up.'

'Okay, what will you give me for Old Kent
Road, with two houses?'

'Fifty quid. Not a penny more.'

'I need the full hundred.' His tactics seemed to
have changed and his lips curved in a wolfish,
persuasive smile.

'Sixty. Last offer. Take it or leave it. If you
want a hundred you'll have to throw in something
else.' They were almost nose to nose, bargaining
fiercely.

Matt closed the gap between them, his lips
brushing hers. 'A hundred.'

'You're going to have to do better than that.'
Beth didn't back down an inch.

He did a great deal better. His fingers trailed
shivery sensations along the line of her jaw. He
nipped her lower lip gently with his teeth, and
when she opened her mouth to gasp, he caught
it in a kiss. 'The property market can be very
volatile. Price can go up at any minute.'

She opened her mouth to speak, but he silenced

her. His mouth was on hers, challenging her to give in to him.

'Two hundred.' She broke away from him, gasping for air.

His eyes were dark, demanding. 'Three.'

He was planting kisses on her neck, his fingers twined in her hair. One hand moved down her spine, finding the tiny knots of sensation, sending warmth flowing through her body. 'You drive a hard bargain.' She had hardly choked the words out when he drew her closer and she was locked against his chest, her hands free to explore the hard threads of muscle and sinew that ran along his shoulders. 'Four it is.'

The game no longer existed. It was all for her now. He bent forward, taking her with him, backwards onto the cushions of the sofa. He seemed suddenly to engulf her completely, excruciatingly gentle and yet relentlessly insistent, his fingers exploring and his mouth taking. She wanted him to take more, give her every last drop of the exquisite tenderness that he was lavishing on her.

'Matt. Matt, wait.' He was suddenly still and she wriggled out from under him, sitting up. 'Not here.' She indicated the curtains, which were three-quarters open to allow the Christmas tree to be seen from outside. There wasn't room on the sofa for him to stretch his long frame out properly, and there was a perfectly good bed upstairs. He could do everything that he wanted, everything she needed there.

'Where, then?'

'Upstairs?' She hadn't meant for the word to be a question, it was an invitation. But somewhere deep inside there was still a knot of uncertainty, which even Matt could not unravel.

He hesitated and she saw a spark of doubt in his eyes. It fed her own fears and was, in turn, fed by them. The escalating passion that had roared between them just seconds ago was replaced by spiralling qualms and distrust. She slid away from him, pressing her back against the end of the sofa.

'Beth...I'm sorry. It's so soon. Is this a good idea?'

What was he talking about? It had been two years, but somehow it was as if he had let go of Mariska only this afternoon. If it was too soon now, then the time would never be right.

'I...I don't know.' She wanted him to persuade her that it was okay, do for her what she couldn't do for herself and break through the barriers that she had erected around her heart. Couldn't he do that?

It seemed not. The Pandora's box of all her doubts and misgivings was open now, and try as she might she could not stuff them back inside and clamp down the lid.

'Then it's not.' He was gentle, but the certainty of tone was back. There wasn't any going back now, no retrieving what had been lost.

He got to his feet. 'Perhaps I should go. I need to get some things done at home.' He shrugged. 'Christmas…you know.'

She knew. There was no point in talking about it—that would only draw out the agony. She'd failed the test—her heart wasn't strong enough to trust even him. And Matt was not going to come to her rescue this time. He obviously had issues of his own to struggle with.

They were both studiedly polite, but the spell was broken. She thanked him for fixing her roof and he thanked her for the meal. He pulled on his jacket and then he was gone, the lights of his car moving slowly down the lane and turning out onto the main road.

Beth carefully collected up the Monopoly board, sorting the money and the cards into order and placing them back into the box. Crying about it wasn't going to help.

She flopped down onto the sofa. She would have given almost anything for just one more touch of his lips on hers, but it was too late now. It had always been too late, even before they had first set eyes on each other. Dammit! Tears rolled down her cheeks and she snuffled into the plump cushions, unable to stem the memories of how good it had felt to be in his arms and how suddenly being alone had morphed into being lonely. Somehow the sight of her Christmas tree, standing in the window, just seemed to make things worse. Perhaps crying *would* help after all.

CHAPTER FIFTEEN

IT HAD been five full days since Matt had seen Beth but he had given up counting, in the sure knowledge that the raw sense of loss wasn't going to be measured by just days. Months maybe. Years perhaps. At the moment he could see himself still thinking of the life he could have had with her when he reached his last breath.

His week had been busy, the last two days particularly so, as the run-up to Christmas and the cold weather took its toll. He'd got through it, though, and so had his patients. The middle-aged man who had required a coronary angioplasty was responding well, and with the insertion of stents into the collapsing artery he could look forward to a full recovery. It was still early days for the woman who had needed emergency bypass surgery, but he was cautiously optimistic.

His phone sat on his desk and when he thumbed it open he saw the expected message. Returning his mother's call, his weariness lifted a little as she told him about Jack's day. Then he sat up straight in his chair, heart pounding. Beth had phoned, saying only that Matt could call her back any time. He passed it off as nothing, a simple message from a friend, and said that he would catch up with her. Then he went to take a shower and change out of his hospital scrubs.

There wasn't much point in pretending to himself that he had seriously thought about what he was about to do next, or that an alternative course of action would have been possible. Matt stood on Beth's doorstep and pressed his finger on the bell, hearing it sound inside the house. He heard a few muffled thumps and then the sound of heels clattering on the bare floorboards of the hallway. The door flew open and he was about to tell her that she should look through the glazed panel before she opened the front door after dark, but she shocked him into silence.

She was dressed in dark-coloured trousers and a jewel-green silky blouse that complemented her colouring. A little lipstick, her hair newly brushed, she was obviously on her way out. But as usual it was her eyes that drew his gaze. Luminous, like pools of silver, beckoning him home.

'Matt!' She seemed surprised to see him.

'I've come at a bad time—I'll catch up with you again.' He had already half turned to walk back down the front path when she stopped him.

'No. Don't go. I was only going to go out for a quick drink with Marcie, and I can cancel. Come in.'

He went to protest, say that she should meet up with Marcie and that he would go home, but he couldn't. Although she didn't move, her eyes drew him in, practically dragging him over the threshold. He was tired. He shouldn't be doing this, he should be going home, getting a good night's sleep and then coming back in the morning when he was rested. But Matt knew that he couldn't sleep until he had heard what she had to say.

'Would you like some coffee?' She was drawing her phone from her handbag and flipping it open with her thumb.

'Yeah, that would be great. Thanks.' He let her motion him into the sitting room and sat down on one of the easy chairs. Not the sofa, that held too many memories. Things that only the determined focus that his work required could drive from his head and which came back to taunt him at every other moment of the day and night. Disappointment, regret and tantalising, heady thoughts of her body under his.

She reappeared with a tray and put the coffee pot and the mugs onto the table. Her phone beeped, and she pulled it out of her pocket and scrutinised it. 'Good. Marcie hasn't left yet. We'll meet up some other time.'

Whatever it was she wanted to say, it had to be important. She had been all dressed up to go out, and now she was sitting on the sofa, rolling up the legs of her trousers to unzip her boots and pull them off.

'All set for Christmas, then?' He thought he would set the ball rolling with something innocuous.

'Just about.' Her face was unenthusiastic. 'What about you? Have you got Jack sorted?'

He nodded. 'I hope so. I took him to the shop you told me about, down by the library, and we both painted mugs for the family. They said they'd have them glazed and ready to pick up at the weekend.' He shrugged. 'Mine weren't very good, but...'

'They'll love them!' Her smile morphed from pasted on to something much nicer.

'For his present, I was going to get him that toy with the fish that all the kids are mad for this year, and I actually had one in my grasp and then put it down again. I've got him a real fish tank instead.' He turned the edges of his mouth down. 'I'm still not sure if that was the right thing to do.'

She clapped her hands together, infectious excitement breaking through the guardedness of her manner. 'I think that's just perfect. Something that you can both take an interest in and do together. Does he get to choose his own fish?'

'Oh, yes.' For a moment, Matt almost forgot what he was here for. 'If he wants to fill the tank with minnows and tadpoles then that's up to him. I'll take him to the shop where I got the tank and show him the fancy tropical fish, but he can have whatever he wants.'

She laughed, and Matt wondered whether that was the last time he would hear that melodic, irresistible sound. Apart from in his head. It was over too soon, and her face darkened. 'You look tired.'

'Yeah. That flu virus that's been going round has knocked us for six. And Christmas is always a busy time for us. Stress, rich food, too much to drink.' Matt could identify with the stress part. Christmas loomed ahead of him like a steep cliff in an endless range of stony crags.

'So I hear. Are you still on call?'

Matt shook his head. 'No, I get the weekend off. I wasn't expecting it, but someone's holiday plans fell through and he stepped in.'

'That was good of him. Means you can spend some time with Jack and get sorted before Monday.' She looked at her watch. 'I'm not keeping you from seeing him before bedtime, am I?'

'No, that's okay. He's at my parents' tonight and I've already called him. He tells me he's got a few secret things left to do tomorrow, so I'm picking him up after tea.'

She nodded silently. It seemed that she had run out of things to say, apart from the thing that she had called him around here for.

'You phoned me.'

She seemed thrown by the shortness of his remark. But he wanted to get this over with and go home to bed. Nothing that she said would have the power to change anything. It was he that needed to change, and if he was unable to, he was damn sure that no one else could do it for him.

'Yes, I did. I've been doing some thinking

and…well, we left a lot of things unsaid and I just wanted to tell you something.' He nodded her on. Tie up the loose ends, why not? Be cool, dispassionate. It was only his heart after all. Nothing of any value.

'I care about you, Matt.' Tears glistened in her eyes and the weight on his chest grew heavier. 'I know that it can't work between us, but I couldn't bear to let you go without telling you.' She seemed to rally herself, wiping the back of her hand across her eye. 'I hope that what's happened won't stop the work that we started from continuing.'

So this really was the end between them. He had expected it, but that didn't mean it hurt any less. He reached for the coffee pot that stood unheeded between them and then changed his mind. He'd be home soon, he would have coffee there.

'I'd like that, too. Sandra Allen's as enthusiastic about the project as I am and she's got more time to devote to it.' He'd make sure Sandra got all the time she needed, so that he could take a back seat.

She nodded. 'Yes, I'd like that. I guess it would be a bit awkward the way it was, with just you and me…' She trailed off, reddening, and Matt's heart banged against his ribs. She was having just as much difficulty dealing with this as he was.

'Allie and the others won't suffer either. I was serious when I offered them my help.'

'I never doubted that.' Her eyes seemed to soften a little. 'I was going to say that I hope in the future some time we might still be friends. I…I've become very fond of Jack and it would break my heart to think that I might not see him again.'

A feeble warmth threaded softly through his veins. 'We'll always be friends, Beth. And you and Jack can see each other whenever you want.' A thought struck him. 'He's getting a mobile phone from his grandparents—why don't I give him your number so he can text or call you?'

She brightened visibly. 'I'd love that. Thank you. Will you give him my number?'

'I'll put it into his contacts list. Or just let him do it, he seems a lot more proficient with these things than I am.'

She choked on her reply and another tear rolled down her cheek. This time she reached for the coffee pot to cover her discomfiture, tilting it towards his cup.

Matt shook his head. 'I should go. I'm dead tired and I need to get home.'

'Yes. Of course.'

It wasn't much of a parting, but at least they had been adults about it. No one was going to get caught in the fallout and they were still managing to be civil with each other. It was better like this.

She followed him into the hallway, and he let himself out, closing the door gently behind him. He could go home now, get some sleep and settle back into his well-ordered life. As he thumbed the remote, unlocking his car doors, he saw the curtains in the sitting room twitch closed, obscuring the lights of the Christmas tree inside.

Despite herself, Beth had run upstairs, hoping irrationally for a last glimpse of him as he drove away. But he hadn't. He'd been sitting out there in his car for fifteen minutes, and now he was striding back up her front path.

The doorbell rang. And rang. She tried to ignore it, but the feedback from her hearing aid was pinging through her head insistently. He only took his thumb off the bell when she marched downstairs and flung the door open.

'I thought that we were going to be adults about

this.' She was quivering with rage, her cheeks tight from half-dried tears.

'Let's not.'

Something sparked, deep down inside her. She was still angry, but there was another emotion driving her now. Something savage and sweet that didn't back off from her desperate need for him. It had taken every last piece of courage she had to offer him the easy way out. If he didn't want to take it then so be it.

'Fine. That's just fine with me.' She moved back from the front door, waving him inside and almost slamming it behind him.

'I know that you won't be like Mariska—' He tried to reason with her but she interrupted him.

'I think that's pretty much established, Matt. No, I'll never be like Mariska. I'm a deaf woman. My father's deaf, my brother's deaf and if I were ever to have children then they could well be deaf, too. But you know what? I'm happy with that and anyone who doesn't like it can go and take a running jump.'

'You're missing the point, Beth. Whoever said there was anything wrong with you, or your children or any of your family? And whoever said that being like Mariska was supposed to be a good thing?'

'Well, you'll have to help me out here, Matt, because I don't understand. What exactly do you expect from me?'

The tension seemed to drain out of him, and he took a step forward, laying his hand on her arm. 'Beth. I'm sorry. Please don't cry.' It wasn't until he said it that she realised that tears were streaming down her cheeks. 'I just want to talk. Really talk, I mean. Won't you give me a chance?'

This was exactly what she had tried to avoid. 'What, so you can give me your list of reasons why you don't want me? I've heard it all before, Matt, and trust me—if you do that to me now, I'll brain you with the Christmas tree.'

'Fair enough.' Something flashed in his eyes. 'What will you do to me if I give you the list of all the things about you that drive me to me knees with longing?'

Before she could stop him he was actually on his knees. 'Get up, Matt.' She aimed a punch at his shoulder that landed with rather more force than she had intended. 'Get up. You're confusing me.' This was all too much for Beth, and she burst into tears, sobbing uncontrollably.

He was on his feet in a second, holding her, and she broke down in his arms. He let her cry, gripping her tightly until the tremors that racked her body started to subside. Finally she took a deep breath. 'Okay, then. Let's talk.'

They sat, staring across the coffee table at each other for what seemed like an age. Finally Matt cleared his throat. 'I've lied to you, Beth. I lied to everyone. But I want to change all that. You made me want to change.'

'How did you lie?' A sudden calm had settled on her. What was this big secret that he just couldn't keep any more?

'When Mariska died, there was someone else in the car. Her producer was also killed outright in the crash. He was her lover.'

'What?' Beth's hand flew to her mouth. 'Why would she, Matt? She had everything—you, Jack. What could have possessed her to do such a thing?'

'She didn't think so.' Beth went to protest, but he held up a hand to silence her. 'Let me tell you, Beth, while I still can. There were other affairs. I knew about them. When she was killed and it was all in danger of becoming public knowledge, the production company hushed it up and I helped them. I didn't want Jack to know.'

Beth stared at him in disbelief. 'You... How long, Matt?'

'It was after Jack's second birthday party. She turned up late, as usual, and done up to the nines, then spent half an hour on the phone in the bedroom. I confronted her about it and she told me. She said that she loved me, and she loved Jack, but she wanted more. She was bored.' His gaze fell from her face and his shoulders began to slump.

'Go on. Don't stop now, I want to hear it all, Matt. I think I may need to hear it.' He needed to tell it as well.

His gaze swept up again and he nodded. 'We didn't argue. If she had shed one tear I would have known that there was something still there to fight for. But there wasn't. We made a bargain. Mariska's new show was just about to go to air, and she didn't want the complication of a divorce just then.'

'And you didn't want to lose Jack.' Beth knew that Matt's first thought would have been for his son.

'She was never there and I knew that wouldn't

change if I left. He'd just be looked after by nannies, with his mother making an appearance every now and then, a new man on her arm each time. The bargain was that she would keep her affairs discreet, and that I'd look after Jack. It suited both of us.' He shot her an imploring look. 'Can you ever understand that?'

'No. I can't understand what she did, Matt. And I can't understand how you found the courage to stay. But I respect you for doing so. You've made Jack's life whole, instead of allowing it to be destroyed by something that was beyond your control.'

He stared at her, as if he didn't comprehend a word that she was saying. 'But I lied, Beth. I've been lying to him and to you.'

'Yes, you did. But Jack's not ready for something like this. Maybe someday he will be. It's got to come from him, though, and until he's ready it's no one else's business. Not the press or anyone's. Certainly not mine.'

'It is your business, though. I let it drive a wedge between us and didn't tell you any of the things that you deserve to hear.' He shrugged. 'But when it finally came to leaving you, I couldn't do it. I sat out there in the car and I couldn't drive away. Not until I'd at least tried to explain to you.' His shoulders slumped again. He'd done what he came to do and he seemed completely drained by the effort.

Comprehension curled guiltily around her stomach. He thought it was his fault. Beth heaved a sigh, trying to goad her lungs into breathing without effort. 'It takes two, Matt.'

'No. No, Beth, don't try to absolve me—'

She cut him short with an impatient gesture. 'You're not the only one who's had a reason to be afraid. I have, too. I was going out with someone…before.'

His head snapped back up again, his gaze searching her face. 'Beth, I've come to realise something. It's not the secrets that keep us apart. It's that we daren't trust each other enough to talk about them. Please tell me.'

He was right. Beth knew she had to tell him, however difficult it was. 'We were engaged. He broke it off, because…because…' Her chest started to heave.

'It's all right, sweetheart. Take it slow if you need to.'

'He broke it off because he didn't want deaf

children. He said…' Beth shrugged, and fell silent.

There was a long moment of quiet and then Matt held his arms out towards her. 'Here. Don't suppose you have a pair of handcuffs on you?'

'No.' She giggled, despite herself. 'Surprising as that seems. Why?'

'Because I think there's something in the Hippocratic oath that precludes finding people and breaking their legs. I might need a little help restraining myself if I'm to do this idiot no harm.' He rose, and perched himself on the coffee table in front of her, taking her hands in his. 'Look, Beth. If there's something that comes between us I want it to be about us. Not Mariska. Not… what's his name?'

'Pete.' Matt's eyes were like pools of deep blue water. Warm. Safe. No rocks lying jagged under the surface. She could trust him. 'Anyway, no leg-breaking. You're just as bad as Marcie.'

'I'll exercise every last scrap of self-control. So what did Marcie have in mind?'

Beth shrugged. It all seemed so stupid now. She didn't care about Pete any more, or what he'd said. 'She wanted to take him out and shoot him.'

He chuckled. 'I knew there was something I

liked about Marcie.' He stilled again. 'Tell me what he said, Beth.'

'He said that his mother had had a long talk with him, told him about all the difficulties and how it wasn't fair on him to expect him to have to look after me and a disabled child.'

'And he listened to her?'

'Yes. He dumped me just before Christmas, last year.'

Rage flared in his eyes and then died again. 'Beth. You can't think… Tell me you don't think that what he did was anything other than cruel madness.'

She shrugged. 'I am deaf, Matt. There's no getting around that.'

'So what? You don't see that as a disability.'

'No, but—'

'If this Pete character did, then he's the one that's disabled. He's disabled because he couldn't see the richness of your culture, and all the other things that make you special. Any child is a blessing, but your children… Beth, your children would be like you. Talented. Beautiful. Compassionate.' Matt stopped for breath. 'I can give you the full list, but it may take a while.'

She was laughing through her tears. 'Yes, but when it's your *own* child…'

'Haven't you heard anything I've said, Beth? If my child was anything like you, I'd count myself blessed. The only thing that Pete did right was to leave, otherwise you'd be married to him now, and I wouldn't have had a chance with you.' He was almost pleading with her. Begging her to understand, to believe what he said.

'You mean you want a chance?' Beth still couldn't quite trust that she'd heard him right.

'Yes. I don't deserve one, but I'm going to ask anyway. You can send me away if you want to but, please, whatever you do, do it because of me. Not anyone else.'

Beth had pulled her hands away from his grasp and he sat back a little. She was going to send him away. If she did, it would kill him, but he'd go all the same. If his heart was going to shrivel and die, it was only right that it should be at her hands.

'What happens if I ask you to stay?' She was nervous, hesitant.

'I tell you I love you. That I want us both to put the past behind us and start fighting for a different kind of future. If I'm lucky, then one day, I'll win you round.'

She was worrying at her bottom lip with her teeth and suddenly she broke into a smile. 'What about today?' She looked at her watch and then her gaze slid back up to his face, half shy, half coquettish. 'You have a couple of hours. That should be enough.'

Almost before the words were out of her mouth, he was on his feet, catching his shin on the coffee table as he went. An empty mug smashed unheeded on the bare floorboards, and he grabbed her hand, pulling her up.

She almost knocked him off his feet in her eagerness to be close to him. Matt crushed her in his arms, a soft, sweet-smelling confection of everything he had ever wanted in a woman. Holding back from kissing her as long as he could, just to enjoy the moment, he felt her hands on the back of his neck, dragging him towards her. She only had time to whisper his name once before he silenced her, pressing his mouth onto hers like a drowning man, cleaving to his only source of air.

He gave her everything. His strength, his passion and all his weakness and doubt. And she took all he had to give, meeting his need for her and responding with an intensity that left him dizzy with longing. There was only one thing that he wanted, and that was the woman that he had in his arms. The closer the better. For as long as humanly possible

Her kisses were everything, but they couldn't fully slake his need for her. All of the nights he had spent alone, before and after Mariska's death, had never seemed lonely. But this one would surely kill him if he couldn't share it with Beth. 'Please, Beth. Will you let me stay?'

'Yes.'

He kissed her again. 'I want to…' He couldn't find the words and so he let actions speak for him, finding the top button of her blouse and tugging at it gently.

'Tell me.'

He wasn't sure how clearly she would hear him if he whispered in her ear so he cradled her face in his hands, facing her. Whispering was over-rated. It was so much more sensual to have her look into his face and to see the emotions in hers as he told her exactly what he wanted.

A shiver of delight shook her body, and she pressed into him, her fingers straining at the threads of his shirt. The urge to get rid of everything that separated them was overwhelming and he pulled at her blouse, sending buttons skittering across the floor. She gasped, and tried to drag the shirt from his back, giving a little huff of impatience when it wouldn't come.

'Wait. You can do that soon enough.' He picked her up, trying to stop his own limbs from shaking as much as hers were, and carried her upstairs.

Beth woke early, wrapped in the warmth of his body with the regular rise and fall of his chest against hers. Even the air seemed to shimmer with echoes of everything they'd done together last night. Carefully she disentangled herself from his arms, shivering at the cool touch of the sheets at the edge of the bed, and pulled on a warm dressing gown.

She felt rather than heard him stir behind her. Turning, she saw his lips move.

'I'm just going downstairs. I'll get some breakfast. The bathroom's through there.' She couldn't hear her own words and hoped her voice didn't sound too shaky.

She was in the kitchen, tugging at the inner canister of the breadmaker, trying to free it from its moorings, when a movement, right on the periphery of her vision, made her jump. Matt's fingers brushed her elbow, and his arm appeared, closely followed by the rest of him. He was bare chested and beautiful, fresh out of a shower that must have taken him all of two minutes.

Beth. She'd taught him how to sign her name last night, and he was already using his limited vocabulary to its full extent. His meaning was clear, though. His open hand held her CI and the hearing aid for her other ear.

She tried to turn away from him, but he moved with her, gently tipping her face up towards his. His eyes echoed the silent question on his lips.

'Okay, okay.' She held her hand up in a gesture of submission and took the CI from him, putting it in place on the side of her head. 'Better?'

'Much. This, too.' He handed her the hearing aid. 'Thank you. I want you to hear me.'

He'd said something of the sort last night, when he'd almost begged her to keep her CI on while they made love. *Please hear me.* And he'd been right. She wouldn't have missed any of his sweet words, not for the world. This morning, things might be different, though.

'I…I need to take the bread out before it burns.'

Beth turned back to the counter top and renewed her efforts with the canister, snatching her hand away as the hot metal scorched her fingers.

'Let me.' He reached around her and flipped the canister out, wrapping it in a tea towel and tipping the hot bread onto the rack. His hand found hers and raised it to his lips and she felt his mouth, soothing her burned flesh. 'What's the matter, Beth?'

'I...I'm afraid, Matt.' If last night had only taught her one thing, it had taught her this. Whatever her doubts, whatever her feelings, she could trust him enough to share them with him.

'Me, too. You terrify me, because I love you. You told me you loved me last night.'

'I do love you. But when I woke up this morning it all seemed too good to be true. I couldn't believe that you wouldn't have second thoughts.'

'I meant every word I said last night.' He dropped her hand and she felt his lips brush against hers. He tasted of peppermint and dreams. 'Should I run through it a second time? Perhaps I didn't make myself quite clear.'

Oh, yes. He could run through it as many times as he liked. She reached out for him, feeling muscle and sinew flex beneath the smooth skin of his shoulder at her touch. 'I think we already did that. The second time.'

'I remember.' His touch turned into an embrace and he lifted her slightly, perching her up on the worktop and moving in close to wrap his arms around her.

'You have no regrets, then?'

'Just one. That I didn't wake up with you in my arms.'

Heat shot through her veins. She wrapped her legs around his waist, holding him tight, tracing the thin, long healed scar that ran across his shoulder with her finger. 'Perhaps we'll have breakfast later.'

'My thoughts exactly.' One of her slippers had fallen to the floor, and he pulled the other one off, tossing it over his shoulder, to clatter unheeded into the sink, with the plates from last night. Gently he tugged at the tie of her dressing gown. 'I think we have some outstanding matters to clear up first.'

'Now that you mention it, there are a few points I'd like you to clarify. Oh!' His hands had found their way inside her dressing gown and her body flamed into trembling desire as his fingers trailed across her skin.

'That one of them?'

'Mmm-hmm. There are some others.'

'Lots of others. We've only really touched the surface so far.' His lips descended on hers, trapping them in an insistent kiss.

'Well, I'm free all day.'

'It's going to take longer than that to cover all the ground.'

'I'll check my diary. When shall I pencil you in?' Beth lifted one of her feet and planted her cold toes against the warm skin of his back and he gasped, jerking convulsively.

'Every page.'

He had her out of her dressing gown almost before she could breathe, and when she twisted the button of his jeans undone he slid them off, letting them fall in a crumpled heap on the floor.

'Upstairs. The condoms are on my bedside table and anyway it's too cold down here.'

He chuckled softly, his lips against the sensitive skin of her neck. 'Ah, sweetheart. I love it when you order me around.'

Their second attempt at breakfast came much later and Matt refused to let her go downstairs alone, claiming that it would be a degree of separation too many. Together they made toast and fresh coffee, then Matt carried the tray upstairs, smoothing the rumpled duvet so that they could stretch out on the bed together to eat it.

They ate and talked and made love. Even showering was too much time apart and Matt invaded the small shower enclosure with her. Soaping each other's bodies turned quickly to long, slow caresses before he wrapped her in a towel and hurried her back to the bedroom to finish what they had started, drawing the pleasure out until it seemed that time had chosen one perfect moment to stop in its tracks.

Some time in the middle of the afternoon, they lay together, talking. There were things to consider—when to tell her family, when to tell his, and most importantly how to tell Jack. Matt wanted to do it all right now and even though Beth urged caution, his confidence won her over.

Beth allowed him the concession of calling his mother to say that she should set an extra place for supper this evening, while she went downstairs to raid the fridge again. When she returned, he was propped up against the pillows, his face thoughtful.

'It's Christmas Eve tomorrow.'

She plumped herself down on the bed, hugging her knees in front of her. 'Yes, can't wait.'

'Are you busy?'

'No I've got the whole day free.' Beth put the bowl of winter strawberries on the bedside table and stretched out on the bed, like a cat in front of the fire. 'I'm going to spend it doing all my favourite things.' She paused as if thinking for a moment. 'All but one. I'll think about that one.'

'What's that, then? The favourite thing you're not going to do.'

'Guess.'

He chuckled. 'That's cruel, Beth. You're going to hide yourself away and leave me all on my own?'

'You won't be on your own. You've got plenty to be getting on with.' Matt needed to spend time with Jack and his family over Christmas, she understood that. She knew he'd be there for her after Christmas and she'd be waiting.

'No good. I can't do any of it without you.' He rolled her over onto her back, suspending his own body over hers on his hands and knees. 'It'll be bad enough spending tonight on my own.'

'We agreed to wait. See what Jack's reaction was before I stay over with you.'

'We did. Doesn't mean I have to like it.'

'Don't you ever need any sleep?' She aimed a play punch at him, but he saw it coming and rolled away.

'I need it. I just can't seem to get around to it when I'm with you.' He sighed. 'But you're right. What do you say we both get a good night's sleep tonight and I'll come over early tomorrow and pick you up?'

CHAPTER SIXTEEN

CHRISTMAS EVE. Dusk was falling and Matt had stoked the open fire in the sitting room into a blaze of light and heat. The day had been perfect. Beth's initial awkwardness the previous evening, when Matt had taken her over to his parents' house, had been dispelled by a piece of characteristically direct action on his part, when he had grabbed her hand and pressed the back of her fingers to his lips. His mother had responded by hugging her and promptly banishing Matt from her kitchen in favour of talking with Beth while she finished preparing the meal.

Today, it was almost as if she was already a part of the family. Matt's father stole her away from him to discuss the pointing at the back of the house and tell her how pleased he was that she and Matt were 'stepping out'. And Jack whirled from his father to Beth like a small tornado, not sure which one of them he wanted to chatter excitedly with the most.

'They'll be gone for at least a couple of hours.' Matt sank down onto the sofa, stretching his legs out in front of him, his arm around Beth's shoulders as if that had always been its proper place. It had been, really. They fitted together as if they had been fashioned that way, right from the start.

'Has Jack taken that piece of plastic mistletoe with him?' Jack had never seemed to tire of pulling the small sprig from his pocket and waving it at Beth every time she came within arm's reach of Matt. She hadn't tired of kissing him, though, and Matt certainly hadn't seemed to mind.

'Probably. I've got him on commission, so he's hanging onto a good source of income.'

'What? You didn't.'

'No, actually, I didn't think of it. Wouldn't have been a bad idea, though. I might suggest it to him next Christmas.'

'We haven't made it through this Christmas yet.'

'That's just a formality. Do you really have to be at the hospital tomorrow?'

'Yes, I promised to go carol singing and I can't let them down.' She was here alone with Matt on Christmas Eve and that was so much more than she could have dreamed possible. And she could hope for other Christmases with him.

'You said…' He jerked upright in his seat to face her. 'I thought you were going to be there all day. The carol singing's just for an hour in the morning. What are you doing for the rest of the day?'

Beth shrugged. 'Nothing.' His brow darkened. 'I didn't want you to think that I was on my own.'

'Well, there's an answer to that. Can't you see how much Jack loves having you here? Don't you know how much I want you with me? Stay tonight. Stay tomorrow. We'll come carol singing with you and then I won't have to let you out of my sight for a moment.'

It all sounded too perfect. Beth was about to ask him if he really meant it, but she could see from his face that he did. Those kinds of doubts were a thing of the past now. 'Okay. Yes, if you're sure that it's all right with your parents, I'll stay.'

'I don't really care if it isn't. But since you ask, if Dad ever finds out that I let you spend Christmas on your own, he'll take a leaf from Marcie's book and shoot me. That's if Mum doesn't get her hands on me first.' He jumped to his feet, reaching for a padded envelope that stood on the mantelpiece. 'And I have something for you.'

'Oh! Matt, I didn't get you anything…' When had he had the time to go out and buy her something for Christmas?

'You're not supposed to. This isn't a Christmas present. You have to stand up, though—here by the tree.' He took her shoulders and positioned her carefully in front of him.

'What's all this?' She looked at the ceiling. 'You haven't got a bucket of fake snow waiting to tip on my head, have you?'

'Nope. Jack and I planned that for later. Here.' He slid a small roll of tissue paper from the envelope and put it into her hand, closing her fingers around it to indicate that it wasn't to be opened yet.

'Beth, my gran gave this to me just before she died last year. I never believed I'd get the chance to do as she asked with it.'

'What did she ask?' There was something about his manner that stilled Beth.

'Gran said that when I found someone I could love, and when the time was right, I should give this to her. And I have, Beth.' He fell to one knee in front of her, so suddenly that she almost took a step backwards. 'Will you marry me?'

'Matt!' Had he completely taken leave of his senses? Of course she wanted to marry him, she'd never been so sure of anything in her life, but... 'This is too much...'

'You don't have to say right now. But will you think about it? I know it's a lot to take on.' He stopped as she laid a finger over his lips and looked at her in agonised silence.

'Too much happiness. It's too much.'

If his grin had been any wider, his face would have split in half. He let out a long sigh and Beth realised that he had been holding his breath. 'Okay, then. Let's take it in stages. I love you, Beth.'

'I love you, too, Matt. More than anything.'

'Good start. And do you want my children?'

'Yes. Blonde-haired, blue-eyed babies, just like their father...'

'Well, there's a problem, because *I* want them to be just like you. But we can discuss that later.' He reached up and cupped her face with his hand, his eyes tender. 'So will you marry me?'

'Yes, I will.'

He stared at her, as if he had never truly

believed that she would say yes. 'Open the package.'

Beth's fingers were trembling so much that she almost dropped it. Somehow she managed to get the ribbon off and unroll the paper, and a heavy gold ring dropped out into her palm.

'Matt! This is beautiful!' The ring was art nouveau in design, gold tendrils wound around three diamonds, which flashed in the glow of the Christmas-tree lights.

'It was Gran's engagement ring. She said that there was a lot of love in it already.'

'And we'll add even more. I'll wear it for her, as well as you. Because she had the sense to believe in you even when you didn't believe in yourself.' She gave him the ring and held her left hand out to him, and he slid it carefully onto her finger.

'Well, how about that? It even fits.' He grinned. 'What more can we ask for a perfect Christmas?'

'Apart from Jack, you mean? And your family?'

'Quite apart from Jack. I don't think he'll give us a moment's peace. Mum certainly won't.'

'Well, as long as he doesn't lose that piece of mistletoe.' Beth giggled. 'That's what I'll have. Some mistletoe, so you'll have to kiss me whenever I want.'

'One piece of mistletoe coming up. Even if I have to trudge all the way down to the local pub and steal some.' Matt got to his feet and put his arms around her waist. 'Anything else?'

'Snow.'

He turned the corners of his mouth down. 'You might have to give that one a miss. It never snows on Christmas Day.' He leaned down to kiss her. 'Would be nice, though. Waking up with you on Christmas morning, snow on the ground outside, Jack asleep in bed, dreaming angelic dreams for an hour…' He grinned. 'Not going to happen, is it?'

'I doubt it. But whatever happens will be perfect.' Beth laid her hand on his chest, unable to take her eyes off the ring. 'I can hardly believe your gran wore it for so long. It looks almost new.'

'The best bit about it is that it's on your finger.' He laid his hand over hers. 'Now, what about some champagne? I put a bottle in the fridge, just in case.'

'Why don't we save it for when your mum and dad get back with Jack? Where are they, by the way?'

'Goodness only knows. I asked Mum if she

could get Dad and Jack out of the way for a couple of hours to give us some time together. Before I could draw breath they were both in their coats and in the car.'

Beth giggled. 'Does she know, then?'

Matt shrugged. 'Well, I didn't tell her, but I wouldn't be surprised if she's worked it out. She's probably got Dad up a ladder in the back garden with a pair of binoculars, trying to see through the back windows, as we speak.'

The front door slammed and they both jumped. Kate's voice sounded in the hallway, calling to Jack to come back immediately, seconds before the door flew open and Jack rushed into the room and flung himself at them.

'Dad, come on—it's snowing. We were on our way over to Gran's and we had to come back, because Grandad said it was a blizzard and that we'd get stuck if we weren't careful. Grandma wasn't very pleased, but he said we had to. It's really thick, come and see.'

Matt swung Jack upwards, his arms around both him and Beth, hugging tight. Kate's head popped nervously around the doorway.

'Sorry, dear. If the weather hadn't been so terrible we would have been much longer than this...'

She broke off as she saw the ring on Beth's finger. 'Ah! Well, that's all right, then. Wait till George hears about this, he'll be so pleased. He's just putting the car in the garage.'

Jack slithered down from Matt's grasp and stamped his foot impatiently. 'Come on, Dad. Tell Gran to stop kissing everyone and come and see the snow.' He tugged at both Matt's and Beth's hands, pulling them both into the front porch. Beth danced out into the thick, swirling flakes, dragging Matt behind her, reaching up towards an almost luminescent sky which was banked thick with cloud.

'What's so funny, Gran?' Jack was wide-eyed, watching Beth and Matt hugging each other and laughing together in the snow, which had already covered the front path.

'Gran. What's so funny about snow?'

* * * * *

Mills & Boon® Large Print Medical

May

THE CHILD WHO RESCUED CHRISTMAS	Jessica Matthews
FIREFIGHTER WITH A FROZEN HEART	Dianne Drake
MISTLETOE, MIDWIFE...MIRACLE BABY	Anne Fraser
HOW TO SAVE A MARRIAGE IN A MILLION	Leonie Knight
SWALLOWBROOK'S WINTER BRIDE	Abigail Gordon
DYNAMITE DOC OR CHRISTMAS DAD?	Marion Lennox

June

NEW DOC IN TOWN	Meredith Webber
ORPHAN UNDER THE CHRISTMAS TREE	Meredith Webber
THE NIGHT BEFORE CHRISTMAS	Alison Roberts
ONCE A GOOD GIRL...	Wendy S. Marcus
SURGEON IN A WEDDING DRESS	Sue MacKay
THE BOY WHO MADE THEM LOVE AGAIN	Scarlet Wilson

July

THE BOSS SHE CAN'T RESIST	Lucy Clark
HEART SURGEON, HERO...HUSBAND?	Susan Carlisle
DR LANGLEY: PROTECTOR OR PLAYBOY?	Joanna Neil
DAREDEVIL AND DR KATE	Leah Martyn
SPRING PROPOSAL IN SWALLOWBROOK	Abigail Gordon
DOCTOR'S GUIDE TO DATING IN THE JUNGLE	Tina Beckett

Mills & Boon® Large Print Medical

August

September

October